Wrong Arm of the Law

"I'll tell you what I told your husband, ma'am," Clint said. "Anyone you send will have to deal with me."

"I will not send someone," Mrs. Locksley said. "I will send several someones. I am aware of your reputation, but you are only one man."

"As I told your husband, I'm one man who will be fixated on you, and on him."

"You don't frighten me, Mr. Adams," she said. "Perhaps you frightened my husband. I rather think you probably did. But you don't scare me. You would not shoot an unarmed woman."

"I'll gladly shoot anyone you send after me, though," he told her.

"Then you'll have to deal with the law."

"You think if you send gunmen to try to kill me, the law will be on your side?"

"In this town?" she asked. "I know it will."

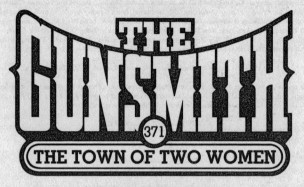

THE GUNSMITH

371

THE TOWN OF TWO WOMEN

J. R. ROBERTS

JOVE BOOKS, NEW YORK

THE BERKLEY PUBLISHING GROUP
Published by the Penguin Group
Penguin Group (USA) Inc.
375 Hudson Street, New York, New York 10014, USA
Penguin Group (Canada), 90 Eglinton Avenue East, Suite 700, Toronto, Ontario M4P 2Y3, Canada
(a division of Pearson Penguin Canada Inc.) • Penguin Books Ltd., 80 Strand, London WC2R 0RL,
England • Penguin Group Ireland, 25 St. Stephen's Green, Dublin 2, Ireland (a division of Penguin
Books Ltd.) • Penguin Group (Australia), 250 Camberwell Road, Camberwell, Victoria 3124, Australia
(a division of Pearson Australia Group Pty. Ltd.) • Penguin Books India Pvt. Ltd., 11 Community
Centre, Panchsheel Park, New Delhi—110 017, India • Penguin Group (NZ), 67 Apollo Drive,
Rosedale, Auckland 0632, New Zealand (a division of Pearson New Zealand Ltd.) • Penguin Books
(South Africa) (Pty.) Ltd., 24 Sturdee Avenue, Rosebank, Johannesburg 2196, South Africa

Penguin Books Ltd., Registered Offices: 80 Strand, London WC2R 0RL, England

This is a work of fiction. Names, characters, places, and incidents either are the product of the author's
imagination or are used fictitiously, and any resemblance to actual persons, living or dead, business
establishments, events, or locales is entirely coincidental.

THE TOWN OF TWO WOMEN

A Jove Book / published by arrangement with the author

PUBLISHING HISTORY
Jove edition / November 2012

ISBN: 978-0-515-15120-6

JOVE®
Jove Books are published by The Berkley Publishing Group,
a division of Penguin Group (USA) Inc.,
375 Hudson Street, New York, New York 10014.
JOVE® is a registered trademark of Penguin Group (USA) Inc.
The "J" design is a trademark of Penguin Group (USA) Inc.

PRINTED IN THE UNITED STATES OF AMERICA

10 9 8 7 6 5 4 3 2 1

ALWAYS LEARNING   **PEARSON**

ONE

Clint Adams was riding through New Mexico, feeling remarkably relaxed in his saddle, when he saw the horse. No rider, just a horse with an empty saddle.

A riderless horse was never good. It usually meant somebody was hurt somewhere.

"Okay, big boy," he said to Eclipse, stroking the big Darley Arabian's neck, "first we catch the horse and see what it tells us about the rider. Come on!"

He kicked Eclipse in the ribs and off they went, after the free running horse.

The animal was loping rather than galloping. It wasn't running in panic, or to or from anything; it was just running because . . . well, it was a horse. That was what they did.

Clint and Eclipse were closing the gap on the horse very quickly. The animal heard them coming and increased its speed, but it was no match for Eclipse. In a few minutes, they were alongside it. Clint reached over and grabbed the horse's reins and pulled it to a stop.

He dismounted and patted the horse's neck, gentling it. It was a mare, about eight years old, a little heavy for running around free. This was not a horse anyone would choose to make a long trip with. Maybe somebody was just out having a pleasure ride.

"Okay, what have you got?" he said. He checked the saddlebags, came up empty. The saddle itself had seen better days. When he looked underneath, he saw why the rider had fallen off. The cinch had broken, the saddle had slipped, and the rider had gone flying. The saddle had righted itself while the animal was running, which was why he hadn't noticed it in the first place.

Looking back the way they had come, he said, "Let's see if we can figure out where you came from."

Clint had been riding north. The horse had come from the east. Maybe the next town.

He held on to the mare's reins and mounted Eclipse again. "Let's go and see what we can find."

He rode east, trailing the mare behind him. He hoped he'd come upon the rider somewhere along the way, and find him—or her—alive.

It took twenty minutes, but eventually he spotted what he was looking for. In the distance, a body was lying on the ground, facedown. He gigged Eclipse into a canter. When he reached the body, he dismounted, tied the mare's reins to the pommel of his saddle.

He walked to the body, got down on one knee, and turned the body over. It was a woman, and she was alive.

He slapped her lightly on the face, but that didn't wake

her. He felt her chest. She was breathing. He looked for wounds, didn't find anything until he looked under her long brown hair. He found a lump that felt soft, pulpy. There were also some bruises on her face that didn't look like they'd come from the fall.

"Okay," he said, "okay, now we've got to get you to a doctor."

She was wearing men's clothes, a shirt that was too big, a pair of jeans, tied around the waist with a rope. A worn pair of boots. He checked her pockets, but came up empty.

"Damn it." He stood up. "What's east of here? Albuquerque, sure, but there's got to be something before that." He looked at Eclipse, who just stared back at him.

"Yeah, okay," he said. "We'll just have to go and look."

Now he had to figure out how to take her in. Sling her over the saddle and tie her, or try to tie her sitting up?

He lifted her, found her remarkably light. The mare would be able to carry her, but the saddle would slip again. He was going to have to figure out a way to tie her to the horse without the saddle. He set her back down again, went to his saddle for his rope.

Ten minutes later he tightened the last knot, then stepped back to take a look. She was lying facedown across the horse, her arms hanging down. The rope was crisscrossed over her and under the horse. He was fairly sure she wouldn't slip off while they rode, but then he had no idea how far they'd have to go.

He had discarded the damaged saddle, saddlebags and

all, since they were empty. There was nothing else on the saddle, no rope, no rifle. She was also unarmed, and there were no weapons on the ground around her. The horse was still wearing its bridle.

He grabbed the reins, then mounted Eclipse.

TWO

The next town he came to was called Heathstead. He didn't know what it meant, but he knew that it didn't matter. The girl needed a doctor, and Heathstead looked big enough to have one. Not a big town by any means, but there was a general store, a saloon, a hotel, a sheriff's office, and a schoolhouse. He thought it followed that the town would have a doctor.

He attracted a lot of attention riding in with a body slung over a horse. He wondered what the people would think if they knew it was a woman.

He reined his horse in and called out to a passing man.

"Is there a doctor in town?"

"Yeah, just down the street, down the alley from the café."

"Thanks."

He found the café, found the alley, and dismounted. Instead of carrying the girl up the flight of stairs, he preferred to find out first if the doctor was in. He went up the stairs and knocked. Next to the door was a shingle that said: DOCTOR R. MATHIS. He wondered why the shingle wasn't at the bottom of the steps.

The door opened and a tall, slender man with gray hair and a neatly trimmed mustache regarded him for a moment before asking, "Help you?"

"Are you Dr. Mathis?"

"I am."

"I've got a patient for you."

The doctor took one step out to look down the stairs, saw the horse with the body on it.

"For me or the undertaker?"

"For you."

"Bring him up, then," Mathis said. "You're lucky. I was about to go out on some house calls."

"Thanks."

Clint went down the steps, untied the body from the horse, and carried her up.

"In here," the doctor called from another room.

Clint carried her in.

"Put him on the bed."

Clint did, as gently as he could. The doctor had his back turned, didn't see that it was a woman until he turned around, wiping his hands on a towel.

He stopped short, then stared at Clint.

"What the hell—"

"Found her on the trail," Clint said. "Her horse had thrown her. She hit her head, but it looks like she had a run-in with somebody before that."

"Why did you bring her here?" the doctor demanded.

"This was the first town I came to," Clint explained. "And she needs a doctor."

"Goddamnit," Mathis said, "go and close the door. And put the horses further in the alley so they can't be seen from the street."

"What's the problem?"

"Just do it, if you don't want to end up dead."

"Well, all right," Clint said, "but I'd like an explanation when I come back."

"You'll get one."

Clint went out, closed the door, descended to the horses, and walked them into the alley. When he returned, the doctor was bent over the patient.

"This is crazy," the man said. "I shouldn't even be doing this."

"Why not? You're a doctor, right? And she's injured. What's the big deal?"

The doctor looked over his shoulder at Clint, then went back to his patient.

"Don't crowd me," he said. "Wait in the other room."

"I need some answers."

"We'll talk when I'm done here."

"Okay."

"And stay inside!" the doctor hissed as Clint passed into the front room.

Clint went to the window to look out. There was nobody at the bottom of the stairs. The only thing he could figure was that the town didn't like strangers. What other reason could the doctor have for being so upset?

He looked around, saw half a bottle of whiskey on a

table with a couple of glasses. He poured a couple of fingers, then downed them to cut the dust. He put the glass back, picked out a chair, and sat down to wait.

Among the people who had seen Clint ride in with the body was a man named Harley Trace. Trace watched as Clint rode to the doctor's office, then watched as Clint carried the girl up the stairs.

Trace went from there directly to the sheriff's office, barged in without knocking.

"Damn it, Harley," Sheriff Pete Crabtree said. "What the hell—"

"She's back!"

"What? Who's back?"

"That girl," Harley Trace said. "She's back."

"What are you talkin' about?" Crabtree asked. "Why the hell would she come back?"

"A fella just rode in with her tied to a horse. She looks hurt or dead. Probably hurt, 'cause he took her to the doc's."

"Doc knows better than that."

"Hey, he's a sawbones," Trace said. "He's gotta treat the sick and the hurt, don't he?"

"Are you sure about this?"

"I'm sure."

"Okay," Crabtree said. "Go back and keep watch. I've got to go and talk to Mr. Locksley."

"Ya want me to get anybody else?"

"Harley, listen up," Crabtree said. "Go back and watch. That's it."

"Okay, okay," Trace said. "I heardja."

Trace left and went back to take up a position across the street from the doctor's office.

Crabtree was forty years old, had been the sheriff of Heathstead for eighteen months. In all that time the only distasteful thing he had done was run that girl out of town. But he hadn't had a choice. Other than that, he'd been able to do his job with hardly any interference.

He strapped on his gun and headed the Eric Locksley's office.

THREE

"How is she?" Clint asked when the doctor came out. Once again he was wiping his hands on a towel.

"We'll know more when she wakes up," Mathis said. "It's gonna depend on how hard that hit on the head was."

"What about the bruises?" Clint asked. "Looks like somebody gave her a beating."

"None of them are serious." Doc Mathis tossed aside his towel, then poured himself a drink. He looked critically at the level of the whiskey in the bottle before setting it down.

"Okay," Clint said, "you want to tell me what's got you all worked up about this girl?"

"You're wondering who gave her that beating, right?" Mathis asked.

"That's right."

"Well," Mathis said, "I can tell you that she got that right here, in town."

"What?"

"And then they put her on a horse and drove her out of town."

"You're saying the whole town rode her out?" Clint asked.

"That's right." Mathis had a drink. "And they ain't gonna be happy that you brought her back here."

"Well, all I knew was that she needed to be treated by a doctor," Clint said. "The beating she took must have left her too weak to sit in the saddle. Also, her cinch broke. She must have hit her head when she fell. I couldn't very well leave her there."

"No," Mathis said, "but you could have taken her to another town."

"This was the first town I came to," Clint said. "How was I supposed to know what had gone before?"

The doctor walked to the window and looked out.

"Maybe nobody saw you come up here."

"Everybody saw me ride in," Clint said. "Somebody must have seen me come here."

"Okay, maybe they didn't realize it was her," Mathis offered.

"Maybe I should go and see the sheriff."

"That won't do you any good."

"The sheriff was in on this?"

"Mister," the doc said, "the whole town was in on it."

"That means you?"

Mathis poured himself another drink.

"Let's just say I didn't do anything to stop 'em." He downed his drink, put the glass down. "I'd offer you a drink, but I'm trying to quit, and I got my intake measured in the bottle."

Clint didn't feel bad about having taken a drink without asking.

Eric Locksley looked up from his desk as Sheriff Crabtree entered his office.

"Sheriff," he said. "What can I do for you?"

Crabtree was careful to close the door. The office was in City Hall, and he didn't want anyone hearing what he said.

"Um, Mr. Locksley, that girl . . . the one we ran out of town?"

"What about her?"

"Well . . ."

The older man frowned and said, "Come on, man, spit it out."

"She's back."

"What?"

Locksley was a pale-faced man with snow-white hair. When he got angry, his face grew pink. It was as pink as Crabtree had ever seen it.

"What the hell is she thinking?"

"She's not thinking anything," Crabtree said. "According to Harley Trace, she was brought in by a man, unconscious and slung over her horse."

"Harley Trace?" Locksley asked. "The town drunk?"

"Well, he drinks—"

"Is he sure?"

"He says he is."

"Maybe she's dead."

"Harley says the man took her to the doc's office. I sent him back there to keep watch."

"Okay, good, good," Locksley said. "Does anyone else know?"

"I don't know," the sheriff said. "They musta rode in right through the middle of town, but maybe nobody knew who was on the horse."

"All right," Locksley said. "Go back to your office and wait. As soon as I decide what should be done, I'll send word to you. Understand?"

"Yes, sir."

As the lawman left his office, Locksley, who owned more businesses in town than anyone else, wondered what he was going to tell his wife.

"What did she do?" Clint asked.

Instead of answering, the doctor poured himself another drink.

"Doc!" Clint snapped. "I want to know what she did to get beat up and driven out of town."

"Why?" Mathis asked. "What do you think you can do?"

"I don't know," Clint said. "Maybe nothing."

"Maybe you should just mount up and ride out," Mathis said, "and take her with you."

"Does she have family in town?"

"No."

"Friends?"

"No."

Clint shook his head.

"Look, what's your name?" the doc asked. "Why do you want to get involved in this?"

"Why do I want to get involved?" Clint asked. "Because

I found her out there. A girl alone who had been badly beaten by . . . by who? The whole town?"

The doctor didn't answer.

"And to answer your other question," Clint said, "my name's Clint Adams."

The doctor stopped with his glass halfway to his mouth, then chuckled and said, "Oh. Oh, that's just great. This should really get interesting."

FOUR

"The Gunsmith, right?"

"That's right."

The doctor chuckled again, then asked Clint, "You want a drink?"

"I thought you were monitoring the level on the bottle," Clint said.

"Forget that," Mathis said. "I'll open a new bottle."

"I'll have one."

The doctor left the room, came back with a full bottle of whiskey. He poured two glasses and handed one to Clint.

"So what are you going to do?" the doctor asked.

"About what?"

"The girl," he said. "Mary. You can't leave her here."

"Where am I supposed to take her?" I asked. "She's unconscious."

"I mean, when she wakes up."

"Do you mean, if she wakes up?"

"Well," the doctor said, "if she doesn't wake up, it'll

be the undertaker's job to take her. But if she does wake up . . . she can't stay here."

"Are you saying you don't want her here?" Clint asked. "Or are you saying somebody would take her out of here?"

"Either one," Mathis said. "I can't have her here. I have to live in this town."

"Look," Clint said, "all I did was bring a sick girl to a doctor's office. I'd be within my rights to get on my horse and ride out."

The doctor's eyes widened.

"You can't do that," he said. "If you leave her here, they'll . . ."

"What? They'll kill her? Or you?"

"Adams," he said, "I can't be sure what they'd do, but I can tell you it wouldn't be good."

"This isn't right," Clint said. "I was just riding around, minding my own business."

"Maybe you should've just kept on."

"A man can't do that, Doc," Clint said. "I wish I could, but I couldn't."

The doctor filled Clint's glass with two fingers of whiskey again.

"She had better stay here for the night," he said. "I figure by morning she'll either wake up, or she'll be dead."

"Then I guess we can make a decision then," Clint said. "I'll have to get a hotel room."

"You better stay here," the doctor said. "Just in case something happens. I got a bed you can sleep on."

"Yeah, okay," Clint said, "but I'll have to take care of the horses."

"All right, but come right back."

Clint finished the whiskey and put the glass down.

"Be careful out there," the doctor said. "Somebody saw you ride in. There's no telling—"

"Yeah, okay," Clint said. "I'll watch it." He walked to the door, turned, and said, "I'll come back as soon as I can." He opened the door, then stopped again. "Which way is the livery?"

Harley Trace watched as the man came down the stairs, went into the alley, came back out leading the two horses. He headed off down the street, in the direction of the livery stable.

Harley ran the other way, in the direction of the sheriff's office.

FIVE

Crabtree looked up as Harley Trace came running into the office.

"What?"

"The fella," Trace said, "he's takin' the horses over to the livery. I guess they're stayin'."

"Goddamnit!" Crabtree said. "I ain't heard from Locksley yet. I don't know what he wants me to do."

"Well," Trace said, "I figured you'd wanna know."

"Okay, you did good," Crabtree said. "Now get on back there."

"Sheriff," Trace said, "I need a drink real bad."

The sheriff frowned, then took a bottle and a mug from his bottom drawer. He poured just one finger into the mug and set it on the edge of the desk. He corked the bottle and put it back.

"You'll have to make do with that."

Trace rushed to the desk, grabbed the mug, and knocked back the liquor. He closed his eyes, then tipped the mug again, to get the dregs.

"I could use another small—"

"That's it, Harley," Crabtree said. "Go on back."

"Yes, sir."

He put the mug down and headed for the door, but he stopped short and turned around.

"Whataya gonna do?"

"I guess maybe I oughtta go have a talk with this fella," the lawman said. "Find out who he is anyway."

"That sounds like a good idea."

"Well, thanks, Harley," Crabtree said. "I'm glad you approve."

Harley wiped his mouth with his hand, nodded, and left.

Clint reached the livery, didn't have any trouble with the man there. He took the horses willingly, didn't seem to recognize the mare. But when Clint turned to leave, holding his rifle and saddlebags, a man wearing a badge was standing in the doorway.

"Hey, Sheriff," the liveryman said.

"Take a walk, Larry," the sheriff said.

"Huh?"

"Go get a drink. Come back in ten minutes."

"Uh, okay, sure."

Neither of them spoke until Larry the liveryman was gone.

"Is ten minutes going to do it?"

"It should," the sheriff said. "In fact, it shouldn't take me that long to find out your name and what you're doin' in town."

"Well," Clint said, "I have the feeling you already know what I'm doing in town."

"Maybe I do," the sheriff said, "but that don't tell me who you are."

"The name's Clint Adams."

"Clint—" the sheriff started, but it stuck in his throat.

"What's your name, Sheriff?"

"Uh, Crabtree," the man said. "My name's Crabtree."

"Well, Sheriff Crabtree," Clint said, "what do we do now?"

"Uh, the girl," Crabtree asked. "How is she?"

Clint decided to tell the truth. It might save them both some trouble.

"Doc Mathis says by morning she'll either wake up, or die."

"Is that so?"

"It is," Clint said. "So I guess the rest of this can wait 'til morning, don't you think?"

"Huh? Oh, yeah, sure."

"Then if you'll excuse me?"

The sheriff stepped aside, but as Clint passed him, the man said, "We'll have to talk tomorrow."

"I'm looking forward to it," Clint said, and walked away.

SIX

On the way back to the doctor's office, Clint passed a café. The smell of cooking meat made his stomach start growling. He decided to go inside and buy two steak dinners, and take them to the doctor's. Since Mathis had opened a fresh bottle of whiskey, Clint thought it would be a good idea to get some food into him.

The middle-aged waitress who took care of him said, "You're a stranger in town."

"That's right."

"Two meals?"

"One's for Doc Mathis."

"Are you a friend of Doc's?"

Clint decided to say, "Yes."

"Well, good," she said. "He needs to have someone make him eat."

She eventually came out with a tray covered by a checkerboard napkin.

"Thank you. I'll bring your plates and utensils back as soon as I can."

"Tomorrow will be soon enough," she said. "What's your name?"

"Clint."

"I'm Amy." They shook hands. "It's nice to meet you. Enjoy the steaks."

"We will."

Clint carried the steak dinners to the doc's, balancing them with his rifle, his saddlebags tossed over his shoulder. When he reached the door to the office, he kicked it with the toe of his boot. Doc opened it an inch, then wider when he saw Clint.

"What's this?"

"I thought we could use some food."

Mathis's eyes, slightly blurry, lit up, and he said, "Good idea. I'm starving."

The doctor made some room on a table for Clint to set the meals down.

"Amy says you should eat."

"Ah, you went to the café. Good, I eat there often."

"Not according to Amy."

"That woman," he said, "she's like a mother hen."

Mathis brought two chairs to the table, then fetched the whiskey bottle and two glasses.

"Might as well kill the bottle with the meal."

"How's Mary?"

"She stirred once or twice," Mathis said, "but she's still out."

They each brandished their silverware and cut into their steaks. Clint found his a bit tough, but the doctor seemed to relish his.

"I ran into somebody at the livery," Clint said.

"Who's that?"

"The sheriff," Clint said. "Crabtree? Is that his name?"

"Yes, that's him. Did you tell him who you are?"

"We introduced ourselves."

"And what happened?"

"Nothing," Clint said. "I think we just agreed to talk at another time."

Mathis took a swallow of whiskey.

"Well, that's fine. Now he knows you're here."

"He doesn't know I'm staying here, in your office," Clint said.

"Oh, he knows," Mathis said. "I'm sure somebody saw you come here, and told him."

"Well, if he comes here, I'll handle him."

Mathis put down his knife and fork and grabbed the whiskey bottle. He poured himself a generous glass.

"Doc, you've got to lay off the whiskey. That girl needs you to be sober."

"Drunk or sober, I'm a damned good doctor," Mathis insisted. But he put the glass down and picked up his utensils.

They ate.

Once again Sheriff Crabtree joined Harley Trace across the street from Doc Mathis's office.

"Are they in there?" he asked.

"Yeah, they are," Trace said. "That fella came back with a tray from the café."

"That fella," Crabtree said, "is Clint Adams."

"What? The Gunsmith?" Trace immediately looked frightened.

"Relax, Harley," Crabtree said. "I talked to him."

"And?"

"And we're gonna talk again tomorrow."

"You gonna tell him to get out of town?"

"I don't know what I'm gonna tell him," Crabtree said. "I'll have to talk to Locksley again. For now, you just stay here and watch."

"Sheriff—" Trace started.

"Don't worry, Harley," Crabtree said, "I'll have somebody relieve you."

"When?"

"Soon."

"I don't wanna go up against the Gunsmith, Sheriff."

"Don't worry," Crabtree said. "You won't have to."

The lawman left Trace there and went back to his office.

SEVEN

On his way to his office, Crabtree realized that the news that the Gunsmith was in town, and had brought Mary Connelly with him, had to be passed on to Eric Locksley. That meant he had to go and see the man again.

He went back to City Hall, found that Locksley had left his office. He'd probably gone home, to talk to his wife. It was, after all, she who had demanded that Mary be driven out of town. Locksley himself may have worn the pants in town, but it was his wife, Angela, who wore the pants in their household. Everybody in town knew that.

The sheriff left City Hall and headed over to the Locksley home.

"She's what?" Angela Locksley screamed.

"Back in town," Locksley said. He was sort of enjoying his wife's reaction. She was a royal bitch and he enjoyed seeing her *not* getting her own way.

"How the hell—how dare she!"

"Well," Locksley said calmly, "apparently it wasn't her idea." He explained to his wife how the woman was brought in unconscious, slung over a horse, and taken to the doctor's office.

"And he is treating her?"

"That's his job."

"Don't try to be clever with me, Eric," she said. "You're not equipped."

Locksley remembered the first time he'd seen Angela, twelve years before. He'd been taken by her beauty and her class. She still had beauty and class, but it was all tempered with her acid tongue, which did not make its appearance until after the wedding. If most of the money hadn't been hers . . .

"Well," she asked, "what are you going to do about it?"

"I don't know," he said. "It's possible she could leave town again in the morning. "On the other hand, I don't know her condition."

"Don't you think that's something you should find out?"

"Yes, I do," he said.

"And when were you planning on doing that?"

At that moment there was a knock at the door. Locksley took that as a reprieve and went to answer it.

"What are you doing here?" Locksley asked Sheriff Crabtree. "I told you to wait in your office."

"I have some more information."

"Important information?"

"Very important."

"All right," Locksley said. "Come in."

Crabtree followed Locksley to the living room, where Angela was still waiting, seething.

"Angela, will you excuse us?" Locksley said.

"Not a chance," she said, folding her arms.

Locksley sighed, then said, "All right, Sheriff. What's your news?"

"The man who brought . . . brought the girl back to town," Crabtree said. "I found out who he is."

"Well, who?" Angela asked testily.

"Ma'am," Crabtree said. "His name's Clint Adams."

"The Gunsmith?" Locksley asked.

"Yes, sir."

"What the hell is he doing here?" Angela demanded. "And what's he doing with her?"

"I'm gonna ask him tomorrow."

"Why tomorrow?" Locksley asked. "Why not tonight?"

"Because he's scared, that's why," Angela asked.

"Angela, please!" Locksley said.

She dropped her arms, said, "We're not done talking about this!" and stormed out of the room.

"At last," Locksley said. "Okay, did you talk to Adams yet?"

"Briefly."

"Find out anything?"

"Not tonight," Crabtree said. "We agreed to talk tomorrow."

"Okay, fine," Locksley said. "Talk to him tomorrow, and then bring him to me."

"What if I succeed in getting him out of town?" Crabtree asked.

"That'll be fine," Locksley said, "but if you don't, then bring him right to me."

"What do I tell him?"

"I don't care," Locksley said. "Just tell him I want to talk to him about the girl."

"All right."

"That's all," Locksley said. "We'll talk tomorrow, too."

"Yes, sir," Crabtree said. He left, feeling sorry for his boss, having to stay there with his wife.

EIGHT

The doctor had a small room off to one side with an equally small bed in it.

"It doesn't look like much," Mathis had said, "but you'll be comfortable."

Clint doubted that, but once he got into the bed, he found it remarkably comfortable. So much, in fact, that he fell right to sleep . . .

The next morning he could hear the doctor moving around. Hopefully, he was examining the girl again. One way or another, Clint wanted to get the matter resolved so he could leave town and get back to what he had been doing—nothing. It had been a long time since he'd had the time to do nothing.

He got out of bed, stretched, and found that he felt well rested. He wondered what kind of bed this was. Once he was on his feet, the bed once again looked uncomfortable.

He washed up in a basin and bowl the doctor had supplied, then stepped from the room. As he did, the doctor was coming out of the back room, drying his hands on a towel. For a man who had killed a bottle of whiskey the night before, he looked remarkably rested.

"Good morning," Mathis said. "Sleep well?"

"I did, thanks. How's the girl?"

"She's stirring," the doctor said.

"What's that mean?"

"It means she's better," Mathis said. "I think she'll come out of it today."

"What do we do then?"

"We'll see how alert she is," the doctor said, "and how ambulatory."

"She'll be able to talk?"

"I hope so."

"I'm pretty sure her saddle slipped and she fell," Clint said, "but maybe she was being chased. The cinch was cut, but if she was being chased, trying to urge the horse on, that might've caused it to break sooner than it might have."

"So if somebody cut her cinch, why chase her?" Mathis asked. "It would have broken anyway."

"Maybe," Clint said, "we're talking about two different people. We'll know more when she can talk."

"Are you going to talk to the sheriff today?" Mathis asked.

"First I've got to bring those plates and silverware back to the café. I promised that woman I would."

"Amy," Mathis reminded him. "Well, while you're there, you could get some breakfast and bring it back. I don't want to leave Mary here alone."

"Because you're afraid she'll have some kind of seizure," Clint said, "or you're afraid someone will come in here and do her harm?"

"Both," the doctor said. "She's in my care now, whether I like it or not. I want to make sure she recovers, even if it's only so she can ride out of town again."

"Okay," Clint said. "What about ham and eggs?"

"Perfect," Mathis said. "Just tell Amy it's for both of us, and she'll fix you right up."

"Okay."

"And try not to get into any trouble until after you bring breakfast back," Mathis said as Clint went out the door.

"Here ya go," Amy said, bringing a tray out to Clint. "Two plates of ham and eggs, and a basket of fresh biscuits. I know the doctor loves his biscuits."

"I'm kind of fond of them myself," Clint admitted. He took a deep breath. "They smell great."

"You better get them to doc while they're still hot," she said. "Bring the tray back later."

"I will."

"Maybe" she said, "you can have a meal here sometime. I can wait on you myself."

Amy was a handsome woman in her forties. Clint could see she'd been beautiful in her time, but even now there was something very attractive about her. Her hair was dark blond, held back with a ribbon.

"That could happen," he said. "Thank you, Amy."

He left, carrying the tray through the street. He nodded to a few women he passed, but noticed them turning their faces away. Apparently, the news had traveled that a stranger had brought Mary back to town. He wondered if he was the only stranger in town.

He made it back to the doctor's office without being

challenged. Maybe they'd get through their breakfast before having to deal with the situation.

"I made some coffee," the doctor said as Clint entered.

Clint set the tray down on the table, set the plates out for them. Mathis poured two cups of coffee and brought them to the table. The two men sat down to eat.

"Plans for today?" the doctor asked.

"Well, if Mary doesn't wake up, I'll go and talk to the sheriff. I'm perfectly willing to take her away from here, leave her off somewhere, if I'm allowed to do that without somebody trying to kill her."

"That may not be up to him," Mathis said. "It's Locksley who makes the rules around here."

"Well, maybe the sheriff has some small influence with him."

"I doubt it."

"Doesn't hurt to ask."

"I guess not," Mathis said, "but you may be asking the wrong person."

"Who do you suggest?"

"The person with the most influence is Locksley's wife," Mathis said. "Everybody knows that."

"Then maybe," Clint said, "I should talk to Mrs. Locksley."

Mathis laughed derisively and said, "Good luck getting through to that bitch."

"Does she know you have such a low opinion of her?" Clint asked.

"She knows," Mathis said, "but I'm also her doctor."

NINE

After breakfast the doctor went in to check on his patient.

"Any change?" Clint asked when he came back out.

"She seems to be resting easier," Mathis said. He poured himself some more coffee. "I think she'll wake up in a few hours—unless she takes a turn for the worse."

"How would that happen?" Clint asked.

Mathis touched his head in the back, where Mary's bump was.

"If there's something going on inside that I don't know about," he said. "Like bleeding."

"You can't tell?"

"I can't see inside her head, Mr. Adams. We'll just have to wait and see."

"All right," Clint said. "I guess I better go and see the sheriff. I'll check back with you later."

Clint made for the door, then stopped.

"You going to be all right?"

The doctor opened a drawer and took out an old Navy Colt.

"I should be fine."

"If that will even fire."

Mathis smiled. "It will fire."

"All right, then," Clint said, and left.

As Clint entered the office, the sheriff looked up from his desk. He seemed calm. The surprise was gone. He'd had all night to come to terms with dealing with the Gunsmith.

"Good morning," Crabtree said.

"Morning, Sheriff."

"I'm glad I didn't have to come lookin' for you."

"I'd like to get this over with as much as you," Clint said. "May I sit?"

"Please."

Clint sat in a wooden chair across from the lawman.

"How's the girl?" the sheriff asked.

"Doc says she may be coming around," Clint said. "She just needs a little time."

"I don't now how much time she has," Crabtree said.

"I can't just throw her over a horse again and take her out."

"You might have to."

"Why is it my responsibility anyway?" Clint asked.

"You brought her back," Crabtree said. "If you leave, I can't guarantee her safety."

"Apparently, you couldn't guarantee it last time either."

"There was nothing I could do," the sheriff said.

"Because of Mr. Locksley?"

The sheriff sat back in his chair, took a deep breath.

"The doctor's been talkin'."

"We shared a bottle of whiskey."

"Ah."

"Should I go and talk to Mr. Locksley?" Clint asked. "The girl just needs time to heal, and then she'll leave town again."

The sheriff hesitated.

"Or is it Mrs. Locksley I should talk to?"

"The doctor *has* been talkin', hasn't he?"

"He told me a few things."

"Look," Crabtree said, "I may be the sheriff, but I take my orders from Mr. Locksley. Everybody in town does."

"Except his wife."

"That's right."

"Then maybe I should talk to both of them."

"That might be a good idea," Crabtree said, "but if I was you, I'd do it separately."

"That's what I'll do." Clint stood up. "What are your orders concerning the girl?"

"So far," Crabtree said, "since you brought her back, I don't have any orders. Not yet."

"Okay." He started for the door. "If you go to the doctor's office and try to remove her, you'll have to deal with me."

"Like I said," Crabtree said, "I don't have any orders to that effect . . . yet."

"Do you want to take me to your boss and introduce me?" Clint asked.

Crabtree smiled.

"I think you better do that yourself," he said. "His office is in City Hall."

"Well, that's fitting," Clint said. "Does the mayor take his orders from him as well?"

"As a matter of fact, Mr. Adams," the sheriff said, "he does."

Clint shook his head. "I've seen powerful men before, but this one controls the entire town and everyone in it?"

"I'm afraid that's the case, Mr. Adams," the sheriff said.

Clint nodded, and left the office.

TEN

Clint walked until he came to City Hall. He knew it would be obvious, and it was. It was a three-story brick box that, he had no doubt, Eric Locksley had paid to have built.

He entered through the double front doors, closed them behind him. In the lobby he saw a door that said: OFFICE OF THE MAYOR. By reading the other doors he correctly assumed that the town's government body took up the entire floor.

He went up the stairs to the second floor. There he found a door with nothing written on it. He approached, knocked, and entered. A pretty woman looked up from her desk and smiled at him.

"Can I help you?"

"I'm looking for Eric Locksley."

"This is his office," she said. "I'm his secretary, Gina Hopewell. And you are?"

"My name is Clint Adams. I'd like to see Mr. Locksley."

"Do you have an appointment?"

"I don't," he said, "but if you tell him I'm here, I think he'll see me." He was sure the sheriff had told Locksley who he was, either the night before or this morning.

"Clint Adams?" she repeated. The name apparently meant nothing to her. He was not insulted or disappointed.

"Yes."

"Please wait."

She stood up, went through another unmarked door behind her. He waited right where he was and she returned momentarily.

"Sir? Mr. Locksley will see you now."

"Thank you."

He passed her, noticed she was very tall and smelled very good. After he entered the office, she closed the door.

The man standing behind a desk was wearing an expensive suit. There was a gold watch chain hanging from his vest, which, no doubt, led to a gold watch. He was tall, slender, in his fifties, although he could have passed for late forties. Some women would have called him handsome.

"Mr. Adams," he said. "Please, have a seat."

"Mr. Locksley," Clint said, "this is not a social call. I think I'll stand."

"Suit yourself." Locksley sat down. "What the hell did you think you were doing, bringing that girl back here?"

"I had no idea she was from here," Clint said. "I was just taking her to the nearest town."

"Well, now you know, and we don't want her here. "So get her out of here today."

"That's not possible."

"Why not?"

"She's unconscious."

"I don't care."

"Moving her might kill her."

"I don't care about that either."

"Mr. Locksley," Clint said, "everyone in this town may be accustomed to doing what you tell them to do. You won't find that's the case with me. The girl stays until she wakes up. Then it's up to the doctor when she can leave."

"The doctor should know better," Locksley said. "I can have someone explain it to him."

"If you send someone after the doctor, they'll have to deal with me," Clint said. "If you send someone after the girl, they'll have to deal with me." Clint approached the desk and leaned on it. Locksley drew back instinctively. "*You* will have to deal with me. Do I make myself clear?"

"I know your reputation, Adams," Locksley said, "but you're still only one gun."

"One gun," Clint said, "pointing right at you. Remember that."

Locksley had nothing to say to that, so Clint turned and left.

ELEVEN

Clint stopped at Gina Hopewell's desk on the way out.

"That didn't go well," he said.

She smiled.

"Not many of Mr. Locksley's meetings do," she told him.

"Why is that?"

"He's not an easy man to get along with." She said this kind of reluctantly.

"Or like?"

"Well," she said, "I shouldn't say this, but . . ." She looked around, as if checking to see if anyone was listening. "Nobody really likes him."

"Not even his wife?" Clint asked.

She lowered her voice and said, "Nobody really likes her either."

"What about you?" he asked.

"Do I like them?"

"Do people like you?"

"Well, I hope so."

"And your boyfriend?"

She looked away shyly and said, "I don't have a boy-friend."

"Well," he said, "then maybe you'll let me buy you some supper while I'm here. You can tell me who else in town is likable, and who isn't."

"I—well . . . I don't see why not."

"Good," Clint said. "What time do you finish up here?"

"Five o'clock."

"Why don't I come by then and pick you up?" he suggested. "The choice of where we go is up to you."

"O-Okay."

"You're not afraid of getting in trouble, are you?"

"Um, no . . ."

"And you're not afraid of me, are you?"

"No."

"Then I'll see you later, Gina."

"A-All right, Mr. Adams."

"And when I come back," he added, "you can call me Clint."

"I will, Clint."

He smiled and left the office, not even knowing if he would still be in town at five o'clock.

"I was kinda worried," the doctor said when he came back.

"About me?"

Doc Mathis looked annoyed. If he was worried about Clint, he didn't want him to know it.

"I thought maybe you had to kill somebody," Mathis said.

"No, Doc," Clint said, "I didn't have to kill anybody."

"Did you see the sheriff?"

"He's not much help," Clint said, "but I saw Locksley."

"How'd that go?"

"He's not much help either."

"Did he talk to you?"

"Well," Clint said, "he threatened me, I threatened him. Is that talking?"

"I guess."

"I did talk to his secretary, though."

"Gina?"

Clint nodded, even though he thought it was a dumb question. How many secretaries did the man have?

"She's a nice girl," the doc said.

"I thought so, too," Clint said, "that's why I asked her to supper."

"You're taking her to supper?"

"I am."

"When?"

"Tonight," Clint said. "If I'm still here. Did she wake up yet?"

"No."

Clint sat down, shaking his head.

"What's wrong?"

"I'm just wondering what would have happened if I'd left her out there."

Mathis smiled and sat down.

"You could no more do that than I could turn you away when you showed up at my door with her."

"I know."

"The problem is," Mathis went on, "we're both good guys."

"That's the problem, huh?"

Mathis nodded.

"The problem with that," Clint said, "is that it makes everybody else the bad guys."

TWELVE

"Hello?"

They both looked up. It was a woman's voice.

"Is that her?" Clint asked.

Doc sprang up from his chair and ran into the next room. Clint was close behind.

The girl in the bed was awake, and they startled her by running in.

"It's okay," Mathis said. "You're okay."

She frowned at him, then said, "You're the doctor."

"That's right."

"In Heathstead."

"Right again."

Her eyes widened.

"I'm back in Heathstead?"

"Yes." Mathis looked over his shoulder at Clint. "She's three for three. That's good."

"How did I get here?" She tried to sit up, but stopped short. "Why does my head hurt?"

"You took a bad fall off your horse," the doctor said.

"Hit your head. This man found you and brought you here."

"Why here?" she asked.

"It was the closest town," Clint said. "And I didn't know your history with this place."

"Well, you know it now," she said. "I have to get out of here before somebody kills me."

"Nobody's gonna kill you," Doc said.

"So you say."

"So I say," Clint chimed in.

"Who are you?"

"My name's Clint Adams."

She frowned.

"The Gunsmith?"

"That's right."

She looked pale, her brown hair was dirty, but when she smiled at the sound of his name, she looked pretty.

"I got the Gunsmith as my protector?"

"For a while."

"How long?"

"Until we can get you out of this town," Clint said.

"And when will that be?" she asked.

"When you're ready to travel," Doc Mathis said.

"And when will *that* be?"

"When I say so," Doc said.

"Well," she asked, "do I have to wait 'til you say so to get something to eat? I'm starving."

"No," Doc said, "we'll get you something to eat."

"You get it, Doc," Clint suggested. "You haven't been out since we got here."

"Good idea," Doc said. "You can answer the rest of her questions."

As the doctor left, Clint asked, "Would you like some coffee?"

"God, yes."

"I'll get you some while you get yourself into a seated position," Clint said.

Clint went in the other room, poured the coffee, and came back. She was sitting up, holding her head.

"Still hurt?"

"Oh, yeah," she said. "Bad."

He handed her the coffee.

"You fell off your horse, and hit your head," he said. "Your cinch had been cut."

She drank some coffee, said, "That doesn't surprise me."

"Was anybody chasing you?"

"Not exactly."

"What's that mean?"

"Well," she said, "when the whole town chased me out, some of them mounted up and followed me. I was afraid they were gonna kill me, so I started riding hard."

"That put extra pressure on that cinch, and it broke," he said.

"So one way or another, somebody tried to kill me."

"Or hurt you," Clint said. "Looks like they did that."

She drank some more coffee, regarded him over the rim.

"Why did you help me?"

"Well, actually, I was helping your horse."

"What?"

"I saw your horse running free," Clint said. "I chased it down, wanted to make sure it was all right. I was bringing it to town when I came upon your body. I thought you were dead. When I saw that you weren't, I couldn't very well leave you there, so I brought you both here."

She smiled at him.

"You're a liar."

"Okay, try this," Clint said. "You were so damn pretty I couldn't leave you out there."

"I could believe that one," she said, "but I don't. You know what I think?"

"What?"

"You're just too damn nice to leave anybody lying on the ground," she said. "Even if I was a man, big and fat, you would've got me up on that horse and brought me here."

"Well," he said, "you got me."

She drained her cup and asked, "Can I have some more?"

"Sure."

THIRTEEN

"How much trouble have I caused you, so far?" Mary asked.

"What makes you think you've caused me trouble?"

She stared at him over her second cup of coffee. Her eyes were extremely blue.

"Come on, the doc must have told you how I came to be ridden out of town."

"Oh, that," Clint said. "Well, yeah, I did have to talk to the sheriff, and some guy named Locksley."

Her eyes widened.

"What did Locksley say?"

"Before or after I threatened him?"

"You threatened Eric Locksley?"

"Well, I just told him that if he sent anyone here to harm you, or the doc, he'd have to deal with me."

"How did he react to that?"

"Not well."

"I'll bet."

"Tell me about Mrs. Locksley."

"That bitch!"

"That's what I hear. Tell me about her."

"She's mean," Mary said. "Born mean, got meaner every day, even after she had a child."

"She's a mother?"

"An accident, I'm sure," she said. "She has one son, treats him like a dog. The way she treats her husband."

"And her husband stays with her?"

"She's got the money."

"Ah. And what do they have against you? Were you trying seduce their son and marry into that family?"

"That's what everybody thought," she said. "I wasn't gonna marry Jake. But he thought so, and he told everybody."

"And his mother didn't like that?"

"She thought I was after her money."

"But you weren't?"

"No."

"And you weren't after her son?"

"No."

"So what were you after, Mary?"

She stared at him, then said, "The truth?"

"The truth."

She sipped her coffee again, then said, "Her husband."

The doctor arrived with her food before Clint could pursue that. He put the tray on the bed so she could tuck into her ham and eggs.

"We'll let you eat," Mathis said. "When you're finished, call us. I want to examine you."

"Okay."

They went into the other room.

"What did she have to say?" the doc asked.

"She told me a secret."

"About what?" Doc asked. "Her and Jake?"

"Not exactly."

"Well, what then?"

"Never mind," Clint said.

"She doesn't want you to tell me?"

Clint didn't answer.

"Okay," Doc said. "Keep your secrets. And keep hers."

"All I can say is things aren't what they seem," Clint said.

"Maybe not, Clint," the doc said. "But you know what I know?"

"What's that, Doc?"

"Things," Doc Mathis said, "are always what they are."

FOURTEEN

Mary called out when she was done. Doc and Clint went in, and Doc took the tray off her lap.

"I'll take this back to the café," he said. "When I come back, I'll need you to leave, Clint, so I can examine her."

"Okay, Doc."

Mathis left.

Clint and Mary sat in silence for a few minutes.

"You don't have to talk if you don't want to," he told her.

"No," she said, "I opened my big mouth, didn't I? I should finish."

"So finish."

She took a deep breath.

"I was sleeping with her husband," she said, "but I let everybody think I was interested in her son."

"Why the husband, if not for the money?" Clint asked.

"He's powerful," she said, "and he's good looking."

"If you like that type."

She giggled and said, "I guess I did."

"Did?"

"Yes," she said, "did. Not anymore."

"Why not?"

"Because he's the one who put me on that horse! Kind of hard to love a man after that."

"And did you love him?"

She paused a moment to think, then said, "Probably not. It was probably the power, the . . . excitement. But no, not love."

"Well, that's good to hear."

"Why?"

"I'd hate to think that after everything you've been through, you still loved him. Especially since I'd have to go up against him if he comes after us."

"Us?"

"Yes, us," Clint said. "And that includes Doc, who could've slammed his door in our face, but didn't."

"Well," she said, "if he does come after us, you have my permission to kill him."

"Hopefully," Clint said, "it won't come to that."

"Why hopefully?" she asked. "You're obviously not afraid to kill people."

"I only kill someone if they force me into it."

"Well, he will," she said, "because he ain't gonna back down—that bitch wife of his won't let him."

"Then maybe I should kill her."

"Good!" she spat. "Kill 'em both!"

"Let's not be so bloodthirsty," Clint said. "I was kidding. I'm not going to kill Mrs. Locksley, but I should go and talk to her."

"You'll see what a hard bitch she is."

"When Doc comes back, I'll find out for myself," he said.

Her eyes were closing, so he stood up.

"I'm going to let you get some rest," he said. "We'll talk later."

"I am kinda tire . . ." she said, and drifted off to sleep.

When Doc Mathis returned, Clint was sitting in his office, waiting.

"How is she?"

"She was tired, so I let her go back to sleep."

Mathis went in to check, then came back.

"She wasn't sleeping before, she was unconscious."

"And now?"

"Now she's sleeping, and that's good."

Clint stood up.

"Where are you off to?" Mathis asked.

"I'm going to talk to Mrs. Locksley," I said. "Everybody seems to think she's got the real power. Maybe I can convince her to give Mary a couple of days to recover, and then leave."

"Good luck," Mathis said. "That woman is not one you can talk into anything."

"Well, I'll give it a try," Clint said. "All I need to know is where to find her."

"Try her house," Doc said, and gave Clint directions. "Biggest one in town. You can't miss it."

"Thanks, Doc."

FIFTEEN

Clint found the house with no trouble, as Doc had assured him. It was two stories, with white columns out front, and balconies above.

He approached the front door and knocked. With this kind of house, he expected the door to be opened by a servant. Instead, a woman who was very unservantlike opened it and stared at him.

"Yes?"

"I'm looking for Mrs. Locksley."

"You found her," she said, "but I don't know you."

"No, you don't, ma'am," he said. "My name is Clint Adams."

"Ah," she said, "you're the one who brought that bitch back to town."

"Well, uh, yes, but the, uh, bitch was unconscious when I brought her back. Not her doing at all."

She frowned at him, then said, "Well, come inside," and backed away.

Clint entered, closed the door, and followed the woman

through a large, high-ceilinged entryway into a plushly furnished living room.

"This is very impressive," he said.

"Thank you," she said. "It's furnished to my taste, of course."

She stopped, turned, and folded her arms. She was wearing an expensive robe that looked to him like silk, belted tightly at the waist. He hadn't known what to expect the way everyone talked about her. What he found was a beautiful woman, tall and slender, although the tight robe did bulge in the right places. She had long black hair, and the skin of her face was smooth and pale. She wasn't evil looking at all, although she was giving him a rather stern look at the moment.

"I am going to give you the benefit of the doubt, Mr. Adams," she said. "You found an unconscious girl and brought her to the closest town for treatment."

"That's exactly how it happened."

"Fine," she said, "now get her out of town."

"I intend to," Clint said, "as soon as she's ready to ride."

"Get her a buggy," Angela Locksley said, "or tie her to a horse again. I don't care how, just get her out of here."

"Mrs. Locksley," Clint said, "you're not being reasonable."

"I thought I was being very reasonable by giving you the benefit of the doubt, Mr. Adams," she said. "I'm afraid that's as reasonable as I can get after what that woman did."

"And what did she do?"

"Never mind," she said. "I don't want to go through the whole business again. It was . . . distasteful."

"Mrs. Locksley, where's your son? What's his name? Jake?"

"That's right," she said. "Why do you ask?"

"I just thought since I was here, I should probably talk to him."

"Well, you can't," she said. "We sent Jake away."

"Away?"

"Back East," she said. "To school."

"How old is he?"

"Twenty."

He'd had trouble guessing Mary's age, but she seemed a little old for a twenty-year-old boy.

"Have you spoken with my husband?"

"I have."

"Were you impressed?"

"I'm afraid not."

"I didn't think so," she said. "I need you to listen to me very carefully, Mr. Adams."

"Okay."

"If you don't get that girl out of town, I will have her killed," she said. "If you get in the way, I will have you killed."

"I'll tell you what I told your husband, ma'am," Clint said. "Anyone you send will have to deal with me."

"I will not send someone," she said. "I will send several someones. I am aware of your reputation, but you are only one man."

"As I told your husband, I'm one man who will be fixated on you, and on him."

"You don't frighten me, Mr. Adams," she said. "Perhaps you frightened my husband. I rather think you probably did. But you don't scare me. You would not shoot an unarmed woman."

"I'll gladly shoot anyone you send after me, though," he told her.

"Then you'll have to deal with the law."

"You think if you send gunmen to try to kill me, the law will be on your side?"

"In this town?" she asked. "I know it will."

SIXTEEN

Clint left the Locksley home, shaking his head. The woman was unbendable in her resolve. He'd now spoken to husband and wife, and there was little or no difference—except he did agree that Angela Locksley had the power.

Mary had told him that she was having an affair with Eric Locksley, but she didn't tell him if Angela knew about it. Did the woman hate the girl simply because she thought she was after her son, or did she know about her dalliance with her husband?

That was something Mary might be able to tell him, when she woke up.

Clint still had not gotten himself a hotel room. He didn't know how long the doctor would let him sleep in that spare room, but perhaps he could go back there now and freshen up for his supper date with Gina Hopewell.

Locksley's secretary certainly seemed willing to talk about her boss, so maybe she'd have something to say that would be of value.

Clint returned to Doc Mathis's office and put the question to him.

"You can stay as long as you want," Mathis said. "In fact, I prefer having you here, in case anything goes wrong."

"Do you think the Locksleys will send men here after Mary?" Clint asked.

"I think if they send anyone, it will be during the night, trying to catch us unaware. Also, that would be the cowardly thing to do."

"You don't have much of an opinion of them, do you?" Clint asked.

"I don't have a high opinion of them or of myself," the doctor said. "Not after what they did to that girl."

"How could you have stopped them?"

"I could've tried."

"And maybe ended up on a horse yourself."

"This town needs a doctor too bad," Mathis said. "I don't think the town would have let them do that to me. But I wasn't thinking that way then."

"Well," Clint said, "don't get too heroic now, Doc. Leave that to me."

"My pleasure."

"I'm going to clean up for my supper date."

"You still have a couple of hours."

"I thought I'd stop at a saloon first."

"I can give you a drink here."

"I'd like a cold beer," Clint said, "plus I'd like to listen to what's being said in town."

"There'll be lots of talking, but nobody will do anything until the Locksleys say so."

"Well," Clint said, "now that I've talked to both of them, maybe they'll talk to each other and come up with a course of action."

"It'll be whatever she says, I'm sure."

"I wasn't impressed with Eric Locksley," Clint said, "but I have to admit his wife comes across as a formidable woman."

"She scares every man in town," Doc Mathis said, "especially her husband."

"Must make it hard for him to go home each night," Clint said, "after being the man in charge all day."

"I wouldn't even want to imagine it," the doctor said with a shake of his head. "I've never been married, but that sounds like hell."

"I've never been married either," Clint said, "and I agree."

He went into the spare room, used the pitcher and basin there to clean up, then put on a clean shirt.

"What saloon would you recommend?" he asked Doc.

"Try the Dry Wash Saloon," Doc Mathis said. "Plenty of big mouths over there."

"Where is it?"

The doctor gave him directions.

"Any gambling?"

"No, just drinking."

"That's very good," Clint said. "I'll see you later, Doc."

"Wait," Mathis said as Clint went to the door.

"Yes?"

"What do I do about food for Mary and me?"

"I'll have something brought up," Clint promised, "or will do it myself."

"Okay," Mathis said. "Mary has got to eat to get her strength back."

"Understood."

Clint left, and headed straight for the Dry Wash Saloon.

Harley Trace entered the sheriff's office and said, "Adams is in the Wash."

"That means that Doc is alone with the girl," Crabtree said.

"Yeah."

"Is she awake?"

"I dunno."

"You haven't seen her?"

"I only seen Adams, and the doc, leaving and comin' back."

Crabtree thought things over.

"Whataya gonna do, Sheriff?"

"Nothin'," Crabtree said, "at least not until Mr. Locksley tell me."

"Then what do I do?"

"Keep watching the doc's place. If the girl leaves, follow her. See where she goes. Then tell me."

"Okay," Trace said, "but when can I get somethin' to eat?"

"Get somethin' quick now," the lawman said, "and then get back there."

"Yessir!"

As Trace left, Crabtree sat back in his chair. What action, he wondered, was Eric Locksley going to take? Or would his next orders come from Angela Lock-sley?

He was getting tired of waiting.

Eric Locksley sat in his office, wondering what his next move should be. If he was going to take action against the Gunsmith, he was going to need at least half a dozen men, maybe more. Where would he find that many men willing to go up against the man?

He stood up, hands behind his back, and stared out the window. He was staring straight ahead, and not down, so he did not see Clint Adams approach the building.

Angela Locksley got dressed in her riding clothes—trousers, a cotton shirt, boots, and a flat-brimmed hat. None of it was expensive; it was all designed for riding or, in other words, for getting dirty. She hated the idea, but it had to be done. There was a man she knew she could send after Clint Adams, but she was going to have to go out and find him herself.

SEVENTEEN

Clint spent about an hour at the bar in the Dry Wash Saloon, sipping beer and listening to the conversations around him. It took a while, but somebody finally came in and started talking about Mary Connelly.

"Didja hear who brought her back into town?"

"Naw, who was it?"

"Clint Adams."

"The Gunsmith?"

"Yeah, him."

"Jesus," somebody said from across the room, "what's Locksley gonna do now?"

"Ya mean what's his wife gonna do?"

Before long the conversation was taking place in the entire saloon from across the room. He wasn't learning anything he didn't know, except for the fact that no one in the room wanted to do anything more than talk about it.

And then there was the bartender. He just stood behind the bar and listened. He didn't take part in the conversation at all. Clint found this odd, since most bartenders had opinions.

Little by little the men talking about Mary Connelly drifted out of the saloon, until the conversation broke down into separate conversations again.

Clint said to the bartender, "No opinion?"

"On what?"

"Whatever they were talking about?" Clint said. "Mary Connelly."

"Oh, that," the man said. "You'd have more opinion about that than I would."

"Oh? Why's that?"

The bartender, a big man in his fifties who had obviously been around, asked instead, "Would you like another beer, Mr. Adams?"

Clint smiled and said, "Sure, one more."

The barman brought it over and said, "On the house."

"Thanks." Clint sipped it. "So you knew me when I came in?"

"I saw you in Yellowstone once."

"That must have been a long time ago."

"Oh, yeah," the man said. "My first job as a bartender."

"And yet you recognized me."

"As soon as you walked in," the man said. "Also, I ain't seen any other strangers in town."

"What's your name?"

"Max."

"Thanks, Max, for not saying anything."

"Well, you weren't sayin' anything," the bartender said. "You was just listening. I figured to let ya."

Clint nodded.

"You find out anything?" Max asked.

"Only that everybody has an opinion, but nobody wants to do anything."

"People around here don't do anything unless they're told to."

"By Locksley?"

"Yup."

"So when they put that poor girl on a horse and rode her out of town . . ."

"They did it because they was told to. And it was Locksley, with a few other men, who actually put her on the horse."

"Ah," Clint said, "there's something I'd like to know."

"Who were the other men?"

"Exactly."

"Well, the sheriff," Max said, "and . . ." Max frowned.

"None of the men who were in here?"

"No," Max said. "Jeez, I can't remember who it was."

"Can't?" Clint asked. "Or don't want to?"

"No," Max said, "I'm tellin' you the truth. It really didn't matter who they were, they was just doing what they were told. So I really can't see their faces in my head. Locksley, the sheriff, and some other hands."

Clint realized what he was saying was true, it didn't matter who the other men were.

"So how much time do you think I have?" he asked Max.

"For what?"

"Before Locksley sends some of those hands against me, and I have to kill them."

"This time," Max said, "I think he may have some

trouble convincing people. He's probably gonna have to hire some guns."

Clint nodded. He actually would feel better killing gunmen than citizens of the town doing what they were told to do by Locksley and his wife.

"You've been a big help, Max," he said.

"I'm a big help in here," Max said, "but I'm a useless shell out there."

"None of the hands putting that girl on the horse were yours?"

"All I do with my hands," Max said, "is pour drinks."

Clint finished his beer, set the mug down, and said, "Keep pouring drinks, Max."

EIGHTEEN

Clint left the Dry Wash and walked to City Hall. He found Gina Hopewell waiting for him outside. She was wearing a dress that was fancier than the one she'd had on that morning.

"I'm not late, am I?" Clint asked.

"Not at all," she said. "I actually left early, went home, and changed for supper."

"You look very pretty."

"Thank you."

"Do you have a place picked out?" he asked.

"Oh, yes," she said. "It's right near here."

"Good," he said. "Let's go."

They started walking, and Clint noticed that Gina appeared a little nervous.

"Did you meet me out front so we wouldn't run into your boss?" Clint asked.

"Well . . ."

"That's okay," he said. "I understand. There's no point in looking for trouble if you can avoid it."

"I hope you're not angry."

"Not at all," Clint said. "Just take me to some good food."

"You won't be disappointed," she promised.

He wasn't disappointed. She took him to a small restaurant on a side street, and if the food wasn't so good, he might have thought she was still trying to hide them from her boss.

"Do you want to ask more questions about Mr. Locksley?" she asked while they ate.

"Well, I've actually found out more than I need to know today," he said, "so no, I don't need to talk about him. I'd rather talk about you."

They spent half an hour talking about how she came to be in Heathstead, and how she got the job working for Eric Locksley. And as they talked, Clint did think of some other questions he could ask about Locksley.

"I know I said I had no questions," he said to her over dessert, "but I have a few."

"That's all right," she said. "Go ahead and ask."

"What do you know about the girl, Mary Connelly, and Locksley's son, Jack?"

"You mean about their relationship?"

"I mean about whether they were going to be married or not."

Gina looked around, but there was nobody sitting near them. She lowered her voice anyway.

"Jack and Mary were never going to get married," she said. "Jack thought they were, but she wasn't in love with the boy."

"Is that the truth?"

"Believe me," she said. "That girl was after somebody else."

"Do you know who?"

"Actually," Gina said, "I don't. I just know she had no feelings for Jack."

"Did Locksley know this?"

"I think he did."

"And his wife?"

"That woman," Gina said, "seems to know everything."

"So when she sent her son away, and had Mary ridden out of town, she knew it wasn't about them."

"Right."

"Then why did she do it?"

"I told you this morning," Gina said. "She's mean."

When they finished supper, they left the restaurant. Outside he asked, "May I walk you home?"

"I'm not going home," she said. "I have some other stops to make."

"Oh."

"I visit some of the sick people in town," she said. "Bring them food."

"That reminds me," he said. "I have to bring some food to some people as well. Should we go back inside?"

"No, not here," she said. "I have a place where I pick the food up. Come on, I'll show you."

She led him to a familiar café, and when they walked in, Amy the waitress smiled at him.

"You're back."

"You know each other?" Gina asked.

"I've been picking up some food here for the doc," Clint said.

"I've got your meals ready, Gina," Amy said. She looked at Clint. "Should I make a couple for you?"

"Two would be great, Amy. Thanks."

A few minutes later Amy came out with meals for Gina and said to Clint, "Yours will be ready soon."

"I better deliver these while they're hot," Gina said.

"All right," Clint said. "I'll see you another time."

Gina started to leave as Amy went back into the kitchen, then stopped.

"I live in a small house on Bennett Street. It's number fourteen. Come by when you have a chance."

"I will," Clint said. "Thanks."

Impulsively, she kissed his cheek, and then left.

Amy came out later carrying a tray covered with a napkin.

"Gina's gone?"

"Yes," he said. "She had to deliver her meals while they were hot."

"You gonna be in town much longer?" she asked.

"I don't know. Why?"

"If you want company, Gina's not the girl."

"Why not?"

"No experience."

"Can you think of somebody who does have experience?" he asked.

"Sure thing, honey," she said. "Me."

"I'll keep that in mind."

As he started to leave, she put her hand on his arm.

"Don't hurt that girl," she said. "Me, I'm cast-iron. But that girl isn't. Understand?"

"I do understand, Amy," he said. "You're a good friend."

Amy nodded, her hands behind her back. Clint left.

NINETEEN

But there were other experienced women in town, and at that moment Wes Tolbert was enjoying one of them. Her name was Annie Jackson. At thirty-five she was one of the more experienced whores in the house. That was the reason Tolbert asked for her. He hated wasting time with younger girls who didn't know what they were doing.

Annie would do anything a man wanted. All he had to do was pay for it. Tolbert didn't mind paying for the things he wanted. At that moment she was on her knees, working on his big cock with her mouth and her hands. She encircled the base with the finger of one hand, fondled his testicles with the other, while working her mouth up and down wetly on him. Every so often she'd take him so deep in her mouth that she would gag herself, and have to come up for air. But each time she would smile and go right back to work on him.

She had long blond hair, which he wrapped his thick fingers in. She was sucking him wetly when there was a knock on the door.

"Don't answer it," she said breathlessly.

"It might be important."

She tightened her fist around his penis.

"This is important."

"It might be work," he said. "When I make money, I spend more money on you."

She opened her fist.

"All right, then," she said. "Answer it." She got to her feet and stretched. She was long and lean, with small breasts and slender hips. He preferred that to women with tits like cows.

He walked to the door naked and opened it.

Angela Locksley looked down at his rigid penis, still glistening with Annie's saliva, and said, "I'm not impressed."

Tolbert looked down at himself and said, "You're a hard woman, Mrs. Locksley."

"I have work for you," she said. "Finish up in here and meet me downstairs."

"Finish up quick?" he asked. "Or take my time?"

"Somewhere in between, Tolbert," she said. "I may be hard, but I'm not heartless. Let the young lady do her job."

She looked past him at Annie, who was still stretching. Something in Angela's eyes excited Tolbert. She reached down, ran the tip of her finger along the underside of his penis, then put it to her lips and licked it. With that, she turned and walked down the hall.

Tolbert closed the door and went back to Annie.

"Get on the bed," he ordered.

She pouted.

"I wasn't done."

"On the bed!"

She shrugged, got on the bed on her back, and made herself comfortable. Annie spread her legs, but when he climbed on the bed, he spread them even more and brutally stabbed his cock deep into her.

"Oh, yeah, baby!" she cried. He started to fuck her hard, thinking about the lady in the hall.

"Wow," Annie said, "somebody sure got you all worked up."

He slid his hands beneath her and cupped her slender ass. She wrapped her long, slim legs around his waist. He hammered her that way, and she moved with him until she felt him grow taut, and then he cried out, exploding inside her.

"Ooooh, yeaaaah," he bellowed, and continued to stab at her until she had milked him dry.

She watched him as he got dressed. He was a big man who looked like he had been built out of stone. Carved, she thought, carved out of stone.

"So when the lady calls, you run?" she asked.

"She's got the money," he said.

"What about her husband?"

"What about him?" He strapped on his gun.

"Do you take his money, too?"

"I take anybody's money," he said. "I'm like you, Annie."

"Like me?" She frowned. "How are you like me?"

He smiled and said, "I'm a whore, too."

He started for the door.

"And the lady?" she asked. "Is she a whore, too?"

"Aren't all women?"

"Have you been with her?"

"No," he said.

"I had the feeling she wanted to join us."

"I don't mix business with pleasure," he told her.

"Then you're not like me," she said, "because I do."

TWENTY

Angela Locksley was waiting in a private room on the first floor. The madam, Lotta, worked for her and kept that room for her.

"In there," Lotta said as Tolbert came down.

Tolbert nodded, went to the door, and entered without knocking.

Angela turned to look at him, a glass of wine in her hand.

"A drink?" she asked.

"Not that stuff."

"I have whiskey."

"Sure."

She turned back to the sideboard, poured him a glass of whiskey, and took it across the room to him.

"Thank you."

"Do you know who Clint Adams is?" she asked.

"The Gunsmith," Tolbert said. "What about him?"

"What do you know about him?" She walked across

the room. It was well furnished with a plush sofa, two matching armchairs, and several tables.

"He's a legend," Tolbert said. "Like Hickok."

"Hickok is dead," she said.

"The Gunsmith can die, too."

She turned to look at him.

"Can you do it?" she asked. "Can you kill the Gunsmith?"

"I can."

"In a fair fight?"

"Do you want it to be a fair fight?"

"I don't care," she said. "I just want him dead."

"Well then," Tolbert said, "I guess I'll assume he's in town?"

"He is," she said. "He brought that girl back with him."

"Mary Connelly?"

"Yes."

"Pretty girl."

Her eyes flashed as she threw her glass at him. He didn't duck, because she was way off target. At worst, a little wine got on him.

He thought about what Annie had said about Angela Locksley, and about her running her finger along his cock. And what she did with that finger after.

He put down his glass and walked to her.

"If you want him dead, it's gonna cost you."

"I'll pay," she said. "I always pay."

"Yeah, with money," he said. "But I want you to pay with something else, too."

"What are you talking about?"

"I think you know," he said. He grabbed her hand, the finger she had touched him with, and lifted it to her lips.

"Oh," she said, her tongue flicking out to touch her own finger.

He released her hand and she touched his chest. With the same finger, she traced a line down over his chest and belly to his belt. She undid his gun belt, dropped it on the nearest chair. Next she loosened the belt of his trousers, unbuttoned them, and drew them down to his ankles, dropping to her knees to do it. When she tugged his shorts down, his semihard cock sprang out at her.

"You're a big man," she said. "And not too tired?"

"Oh, no," he said. "Not at all."

She took his cock in her hand and stroked it until it was fully hard. She ran her nose up and down the length of him, breathing in his scent, then ran her tongue along the same area. Finally, she took him into her mouth and began to suck.

Maybe Annie was right, he thought. Maybe she would join them next time . . .

TWENTY-ONE

Clint entered the doctor's office with the tray.

"I could get used to this," Doc Mathis said. "Having my meals brought to me by the famous Gunsmith."

"I'll take Mary's in to her," Clint said. "How is she?"

"A lot better. Food will help."

Clint poured a cup of coffee, put it on the tray, and carried it into the other room.

"There you are," she said from the bed. "I'm starving."

"Sorry," he said. "I was . . . occupied."

He carried the tray to the bed and set it on her lap. He removed the napkin with a flourish, revealing a steaming bowl of beef stew.

"It smells great," she said. "This from the café?"

"Yes."

"Good food there," she said. "That's all I was gonna miss when I left here."

She tucked into the stew and Clint went back to the other room, where Doc was doing the same.

"Whiskey?" Doc asked.

Clint held up his hand. "I've had more whiskey in the past few days than I've had in a month. I prefer beer."

"You find out anything interesting?"

"A bartender named Max recognized me," Clint said.

"I know Max," Doc said. "He's a good man."

"He wasn't on the street when they rode Mary out?" Clint asked.

"No, he wasn't," Doc said, "but like me, there wasn't much he could do about it."

"What kind of guns have the Locksleys got on their payroll?"

"If you're smart," Doc said, "you'll look at those two as very separate dangers. Either one of them can use money to send some guns your way. The more money, the better the guns."

"That's not always the case, Doc," Clint said, "but I take your point."

Clint sat.

"So what do we do now?" Doc asked.

"We keep that girl alive," Clint said. "I think Mrs. Locksley is just crazy enough to have her killed."

"Well," Doc said, "they know where she is."

"Yeah," Clint said, "and that's a problem."

"So we've got to move her."

"Yeah," Clint said, "but where to? Are there any other people in town who might help?"

"I'll have to think about that," Doc said. "Everybody pretty much kowtows to the Locksleys."

"There must be somebody we can put her with who'll keep an eye on her until she can travel."

"I'll think about it."

"I had supper with Gina Hopewell tonight."

"Nice girl," he said. "Too bad she works for Locksley."

"She doesn't like him very much."

"Nobody does."

"What about her?" Clint asked. "What if I asked her to take Mary in?"

"Why would she want that kind of trouble?" Doc asked.

"Then what about the waitress? Amy?"

"She's a nice woman," Doc said. "She doesn't need that kind of trouble either."

"I suppose not. What about a man? The sheriff?"

"No, not him," Doc said.

"I didn't think so. What about somebody we could hire?"

"Hire?" he asked. "We?"

"Me," Clint said. "Anybody I could hire? I mean, if the Locksleys can hire somebody, so could I."

"You want to hire some guns?"

"If I needed guns," Clint said, "I wouldn't have to hire any. I've got friends I could send for."

"Then maybe you should do that," Doc said. "Ask some of your friends to come and help."

Clint rubbed the back of his neck.

"I got myself into this," Clint said. "I don't think I've got the right to ask my friends to put their lives on the line for Mary."

"You're doing it," Doc said.

"So are you, Doc," Clint said. "Why?"

Doc shrugged.

"I should've tried to help her before," he said. "I guess

I'll try now. I'll keep giving it some thought. Maybe I can come up with somebody who'll take her in."

"Gina and Amy," Clint said, "they're the nicest people I've met in town. So I think I'll ask them if they can think of anybody."

"Good idea," Doc said. "Give Mary and me time to finish this stew, and you can go back to the café and talk to Amy."

"I think I'll do that," Clint said. He settled back in his chair and watched the older man finish his supper.

TWENTY-TWO

Tolbert pulled his pants back up. Angela Locksley stepped back, ran her fingers around her mouth to make sure she was clean.

"Is that what you had in mind?" she asked.

"That," he said, "and money."

"You'll get your money," she said.

"Half before," Wes Tolbert said, "and half after."

"Okay."

"Does your husband know about this?"

"No," she said, "he doesn't know anything. He's useless."

She turned to look at him, then closed on him and took hold of his arms.

"I need a man who can get things done, Wes," she said. "Are you that man?"

He smiled at her.

"I just had you on your knees, didn't I?" he asked.

She smiled and said, "You want me on my back?"

"You know it."

"Then you're my man," she said, squeezing his arm.

*   *   *

Clint walked back to the café, which was empty by the time he got there. Amy was sitting at a back table, waiting to see if any customers would come late. Clint didn't smell anything cooking.

"Brought back your things," he said.

"Thank you."

She took the plates, forks, knives, and tray from him, and set them aside.

"I don't smell anything cooking."

"The cook's gone," she said.

"What happens if somebody comes in and wants to eat?" he asked.

"Then I cook."

"Expecting anybody?" he asked.

She walked to the front doors, locked them, turned the sign hanging there so that it said CLOSED on the outside, then pulled the shades down. Then she turned to look at him, her hands behind her back.

"I was expecting you."

"Were you?"

She nodded, walked toward him. She took her hands from behind her back and put them against his chest.

"Are you going to see Gina tonight?" she asked.

"Probably not."

"Good." She leaned in and kissed him, She smelled of fried foods and something else. He grabbed her, kissed her back. "I don't like to share."

"Me neither," he said.

Her body was solid inside her cheap dress. He took

her apron off, lifting it over her head. She kept her hands up, so he followed with the dress. She was naked underneath. The smell of her sweat came from her armpits, not unpleasant. Her breasts were full, with heavy undersides and dark nipples. The tangle of hair between her thighs was darker than the blond hair on her head. He pulled away the ribbon that held it at the back of her neck, and her long hair fell free.

He put his arms around her, enjoying the solid feel of her against his body. Her skin was hot as he pulled her closer and kissed her again, mashing her breasts up against his chest.

She moaned into his mouth as his hands traveled down her back and cupped her buttocks. One of her hands slid between them, cupping his crotch. What she found there interested her.

She broke the kiss, pushed him back until the backs of his thighs banged against a table. He sat on it awkwardly, and she unbuttoned his pants and freed his hard penis. She stroked it with one hand, pulled on it, then went for his gun belt. He pushed her hands away and removed it himself, laid it within arm's reach. He let her do the rest, until she was on her knees in front of him, and his trousers and shorts were pooled around his ankles. She took his cock in her mouth and lovingly sucked it. She rubbed his thighs and his calves while continuing to suckle him, making wet sounds as her mouth moved up and down on him.

Eventually he put his hands beneath her arms and lifted her to her feet. He turned, set her down on the table, spread her thighs, and pressed his penis against her. He rubbed it along her wet slit, and then entered her quickly, cleanly.

She gasped, clutched him to her with her arms, and wrapped her legs around his waist. As he pumped his cock into her, the table jumped beneath them, and neither of them saw the eyes that were peering at them from beneath the shade . . .

Harley Trace watched as Clint Adams fucked the waitress—what was her name? Amy, yeah, that was it. It looked to him like the table they were on wasn't going to hold. He was waiting for it to fall apart beneath them.

He took his eyes from the window, looked around to be sure nobody was watching him. There were some women across the street, walking, so he had to move before they saw him.

He left the front of the café, crossed the street, found a doorway, and waited there . . .

"Oh, Jesus," Amy said into his ear.
   "What?"
   She laughed.
   "I think I got a splinter in my ass."
   "Want me to stop?"
   "Oh, God, no," she said, raking his back with her nails.
   He slid his hands beneath her ass, between her and the wooden table, to keep her from getting another splinter, and continued to fuck her. Her breath came hard in his ears, sweet puffs of air. She was sweating, but it was different from the perspiration that had already dried on her.

This felt different, smelled different . . . when he licked her shoulders, and the slopes of her breasts, bit her neck, it tasted different.

"I have a bed in the back," she said.

"You own this place?" he asked.

"Yes."

"Then take me there," he said. He lifted her in his arms.

TWENTY-THREE

The bed was small, the mattress thin, but it offered more comfort than a restaurant table.

He made love to her once, then fucked her once. They were two different things, both glorious. Afterward, Clint and Amy lay together in her bed, their sweat cooling.

"What are you gonna do now?" she asked.

"I still have to find a safe place for Mary," he said.

"You know they'll try to kill her if you don't get her out of town."

"Yes."

"Then why don't you leave tonight?"

"She can't ride," he said. "She needs a couple of days."

"And you need a place to hide her, 'cause they know she's at Doc's."

"Right."

"Is that what this was about?" she asked.

"No," he said. "I didn't know you'd be waiting for me . . . like this."

"Then what?"

"I wouldn't ask you," he said.

"Why not?"

"I wouldn't want to put you at risk," he said. "Besides, there's no room here."

She rolled over and looked at him.

"I have a house, a small one, outside of town," she said. "Nobody knows about it. It's been closed up for a while. Take her there."

"Why?"

"Why not?" she asked. "I want to help. She got a raw deal, didn't deserve to be run out of town."

"Where were you when it happened?"

"In here," she said, "serving steaks."

He sat up.

"Are you going?"

"I've got to get Mary away from Doc's," he said.

"Your clothes are in the café," she reminded him as he looked around.

"Oh, yeah," he said. He realized his gun was there, too. Not a smart thing to do. He could have been dead by now.

Stupid.

"Come on," she said, getting out of bed. "Let's get dressed and I'll show you the house."

Harley Trace watched as Clint and Amy came out the front door of the café. They started to walk away, but then abruptly Clint Adams stopped, and started across the street.

In a panic, Trace's feet would not move.

"Hold on a second," Clint said to Amy. "I have to talk to someone."

"Who?"

"Just wait."

He stepped into the street to cross to the other side. The man he was approaching saw him, but seemed incapable of moving.

When Clint reached him, the man looked as if he was going to cry, or faint.

"What's your name?" Clint asked.

"Ha-Ha-Harley T-Trace."

"You've been watching me since I got to town, Harley," Clint said. "Why?"

"I—I—I was told to."

"By who? Eric Locksley?"

"Oh, no, sir," Trace said. "I'm, uh, workin' for the sheriff."

"And what does he want you to do?" Clint asked.

"J-Just keep an eye o-on you."

"And the girl?"

"Y-Yeah."

"Well," Clint said, "I think you're done for the day, Harley."

"Um, the sheriff said—"

"Never mind what the sheriff said," Clint cut him off. "You're done."

"B-But w-what—"

Trace had all the indications of being an alcoholic. Clint took some money from his pocket.

"Go and get yourself a drink or two," Clint said, putting the coins in Harley's pocket. "Then, in a little while, come to the doc's. I'll be back there again."

"But—"

"The sheriff never has to know," Clint said. "Go. Otherwise I'm going to have to hurt you. Wouldn't you rather have a couple of drinks?"

"Well, yeah."

"Then go," Clint said. "I'll see you later."

Clint started back across the street.

"Mr. Adams?"

Clint turned.

"What?"

"You seen me right from the beginnin'?" Harley asked.

"Right from the start, Harley."

"Jeez," Harley said as the Gunsmith went back across the street. He swallowed hard as he realized the Gunsmith could have killed him anytime he wanted to.

"What was that about?" Amy asked.

"He's been watching me since I got to town."

"Harley? He's usually only worried about his next drink."

"Well, seems like the sheriff's got him on a short leash while he's watching me."

"What did you do?"

"Gave him some money."

"He'll go get drunk," she said. "He'll be in a lot of trouble with the sheriff."

"I told him I'd be at Doc's later, and to meet me there," Clint said. "The sheriff won't hear from me that he went for a few drinks."

"I hope he doesn't hear it from anybody."

"Let's make this quick," he said, "and nobody will have to get into trouble."

"Okay," she said. "This way."

TWENTY-FOUR

The house was small, and musty from having been closed up for so long. Amy led Clint there as it was getting dark. Once there, she opened the door, and lit a lamp that was hanging on the wall.

"There's not much here anymore," she said. "A chair, a cot. There's a stream out back where you can get fresh water. I think there's still a bucket."

Clint looked around. The house had only two rooms. There was an old stove against one wall.

"The stove might still work if you put some wood in it."

"She won't be here long enough to want to cook," Clint said. "But this will do."

"You want to bring her here tonight?" Amy asked.

"I'll go back and see if she can walk," he said. "If I need a buckboard, it'll have to wait until tomorrow."

"I have a buggy behind the café," Amy said. "I can bring her here."

"You've done enough—"

"Tonight's the time to do this," Amy said. "You made sure that Harley will be drunk. No one's watching."

"The danger—"

"We should stop arguing and go do it now, Clint."

Clint stared at her, saw in her face that she would not be deterred.

"All right," he said. "Let's go."

Clint went back to the doctor's office while Amy went to fetch the buggy. Before he went inside, he looked around. No one was watching.

As soon as the doctor opened the door, he asked, "Where have you bee—"

"Can she walk?" Clint asked Mathis.

"I suppose so," the doc said, "but she shouldn't ride."

"Amy's bringing a buggy around," Clint said. "I have a place to take Mary to keep her safe."

"Where?"

"The less you know, the better."

"I still have to treat her."

"I'll come and get you, and bring you to her," Clint said. "For now, just help me get her down the stairs and into the buggy."

With Clint on one side and Mathis on the other, they walked her down the stairs. She was wearing the dirty clothes she'd had on when Clint found her.

Amy was waiting with a buggy, as promised.

"Amy," Mary said. "Why are you doin' this?"

"I just want to help, Mary."

Mary didn't seem to know how to respond, but finally she just said, "Thanks."

Clint and Doc lifted her onto the seat next to Amy.

"Take her out there," Clint said. "I'll be along."

"We'll be fine," Amy said. She looked at Mary. "I brought you some clean clothes. And we can give you a bath."

"Oh, I'd love a bath!" Mary said.

Amy looked at Clint.

"By the time you join us," she said, "you won't recognize her."

"I'll look forward to it."

He slapped the horse on the rump and they rode into the darkness.

"Is she taking her to her old house, outside of town?" Doc asked.

Clint asked, "You know about that?"

"I do."

"Well, hopefully the Locksleys won't think of it."

They went back up the stairs and into Doc's place.

"There's been a man watching us since we arrived," Clint told him.

"What? Who?"

"Harley Trace."

The doctor looked relieved.

"For a minute you scared me," he said.

"Why aren't you scared?"

"Harley's a drunk."

"I figured that, so I gave him some money. But he'll be back here soon."

"Why is he watching us?"

"He says the sheriff told him to."

"That's bad," Doc said. "If the sheriff has been watching us, it's for Locksley."

"Well," Clint said, "maybe he has him watching me, not you. We'll find out when I leave here."

"Where are you going?" the doc asked.

"I'll stay with Mary at Amy's house."

"I'll come out there to treat her," Doc said, "and make sure I'm not followed."

"Okay," Clint said. "Trace might be back here any minute."

"I doubt it," Doc said. "He's probably crawled into a bottle."

"I didn't give him that much money," Clint said. "A couple of drinks at best."

"He'll get somebody else to buy him a drink," Doc said.

"Just in case," Clint said, "I'll get out of here now."

"Go," Doc said. "I'll see you tomorrow."

Clint nodded, said, "Thanks, Doc."

He left, went down the stairs, and stopped. He looked around, didn't see Trace or anyone else. Instead of walking on the street, he melted into the darkness of the alley, walked through to the other side, leading Eclipse. He used back streets to get to the end of town, then walked to Amy's house.

When he got there, he saw the light from the lamp inside. They were going to have to cover the windows to block that light, but the house would do.

For a while.

TWENTY-FIVE

"You came too soon," Amy said. "We're still getting her cleaned up."

She backed away to let him enter.

"She's in the other room."

"I want to cover the windows, so nobody will see the lights."

"I think I have some old blankets," she said. "You can tear them apart to use as shades. Wait here."

She went into the other room, opening the door to enter. Clint caught a glimpse of a naked Mary, washing herself with a bucket of water. It was just a quick glimpse, but he saw a full, round breast and a dark pubic bush before Amy closed the door.

Amy came back out, carrying some blankets.

"I hope this will be enough," she said. "If not, I can come back with more tomorrow."

"I'll cover the front windows," Clint said. "We won't have to cover the back if we keep the door closed."

"Okay."

"When I'm done with this, I'm going to see to my horse," Clint said. He felt bad that Eclipse had not been unsaddled and properly brushed and fed.

"By the time you finish all that, she'll be ready to be seen," Amy said.

Clint nodded. As she went back into the room, he began tearing the blankets.

When the sheriff walked into the saloon and saw Harley Trace at the bar, he couldn't believe his eyes.

"Jesus," he said.

Trace was leaning on the bar, clearly drunk. He was begging the bartender for another drink.

"Come on, Ernie," he said. "One more."

"You've had your drinks, Harley," Ernie said. "Your money's gone."

The sheriff approached and clapped his hand on Harley's left shoulder.

"Ow!" The drunk turned and his eyes widened when he saw the lawman. "Sheriff. Buy me a drink—"

"Are you crazy?" Sheriff Crabtree said. He dragged Harley outside, then let him go. The man staggered.

"What the hell are you doing in the saloon? I told you to watch Adams."

"B-But . . . he gave me some money."

"He did, huh? And where is he?"

"He's—he's at Doc's."

"Let's go and see, Harley," Crabtree said. "You better hope he is there."

"How about one more drink before he go—"

"Come on!" Crabtree grabbed Harley and pushed him ahead of him.

"Hello, Sheriff," Doc Mathis said.

"Doc. Can we come in?"

"Sure." Mathis backed away from the door to let Crabtree and Harley enter.

"Doc, is Clint Adams here?"

"He was."

"And the Connelly girl?"

"She was here, too."

"Where are they now?"

"Gone."

"Gone where?"

Doc shrugged. "Adams said you wanted him and the girl gone, so they left."

"Left town?"

"I don't know, Sheriff. All I know is that they're not here."

"Mind if I have a look?"

"Go ahead."

"Give Harley a seat, Doc."

"Here." The doc pulled a chair over for Harley to sit in.

"How about a drink, Doc?" Harley asked.

"Sorry, Harley," Mathis said. "You've had enough."

The sheriff looked in the other rooms. The beds were made, as if they hadn't been used in some time. Nobody was around. He came back out.

"This is no good, Doc," he said. "Locksley's not gonna like it."

"I thought he wanted them gone."

"He wanted them kept track of, until they did leave," Crabtree said.

"I wanna drink!" Harley whined.

"You're in a lot of trouble, Harley," Crabtree said.

"I ain't a deputy, Sheriff," Harley said. "Ya shouldn'ta made me watch."

"Let's go," Crabtree said. He pulled Harley out of the chair and pushed him to the door. "This ain't over, Doc."

"It's over for me," Mathis said. "I treated the girl and she's gone."

"We'll see, Doc," Crabtree said. "We'll see."

TWENTY-SIX

Clint finished rubbing Eclipse down with a cloth he made from a blanket. He didn't have any feed for the animal, but he walked down to the brook and found some fresh grass.

"Best I can do for now, big boy," he said. He left Eclipse behind the house and went back inside, with his saddlebags and rifle. Amy and Mary were still in the other room.

He walked to the stove, wondering if he'd be able to use it to make some coffee. He was about to go out and get some wood when the door opened and Amy stepped out.

"Okay," she said, "she's all cleaned up, and wearing one of my dresses."

Mary came out, and Clint was stunned. The dress was blue, made her eyes even bluer. Her hair was clean and brushed, hanging down past her shoulders. Her age had been hard to determine when she was grimy, but now she looked about twenty-five.

"Wow," he said. "What a difference. You're beautiful."

"Thank you."

"Being clean works wonders for a girl's looks," Amy said.

"That and a dress," Mary said. "Thank you so much, Amy . . . for everything."

"Don't mention it," Amy said. "I better get going. I have to get the buggy back to the stable and take care of the horse. Then I need to get some sleep so I can open early tomorrow."

"I appreciate everything, Amy," Clint said.

"Walk me to the buggy, Clint," Amy suggested.

"Okay." To Mary he said, "I'll be right back."

He and Amy left the house and walked to the buggy.

"She's real fragile right now, Clint," Amy said. "You better take it easy with her."

"I have been."

"I think you can get a fire going in that stove and make some coffee."

"I can do that, but I don't want any smoke coming from the chimney. I'll figure something out."

He helped Amy up into her seat, and she picked up her reins.

"I'll be at the café if you need me," she said.

"I won't want to wake you," he said. "I'm sure we'll be okay."

"I'll stop by tomorrow," she said, and shook the reins at her horse. As she rode away, Clint went back to the house.

Mary was peering into the stove.

"Coffee sound good, but what about the smoke coming from the chimney?"

"We can risk it tonight," he said, "but not during the day. I'll go and get some wood."

"Good," she said. "Maybe the stove will also warm it up in here."

It wasn't that cold, so maybe she was feeling it for a different reason.

He went out and came back with an armful of kindling.

When he got the fire going, he went out again for water, and put the pot on the stove to boil.

There were two chairs, so they pulled them over by the stove and sat down.

"How are you feeling?" he asked.

"I have a headache, otherwise I'm okay," she said.

"We'll find out from Doc when you can ride, and get you out of here," Clint said.

"Then I'll be back where I started," she said, "on a horse with no money, and no place to go."

"Not quite," he said. "We'll get you a good horse and a good saddle, and we'll figure out a place for you to go."

"Why are you being so helpful?"

"Well, I'm the one who put you in danger again by bringing you back to this town."

"Yeah, but you also saved my life by not leaving me out there."

"I just want to help you get away from here," Clint said, "then you can be on your own."

"You think they'll let me leave again?"

"Why not? All they want is for you to go away."

"Actually," she said, "I think Angela wanted me dead. It was Eric who chased me out of town."

"I'll just try to keep them both away from you."

"This is my own fault," she said. "I should have left town on my own a long time ago. I was just so . . . caught up in . . . everything."

"A powerful, rich man who's interested in you, I guess that's pretty hard to walk away from."

"Not if you have self-respect," she said. "I guess I didn't have any."

"You can get some," Clint said. "Leave here, get yourself set up in a new town, with a new life."

"You make it sound so easy."

"It can be," Clint said. "But it all starts with getting you away from here."

"Well, I'm all for that." Mary looked around at the windows, which were covered with bits of blankets. "Are there any blankets left?"

"There's one I didn't cut up," he said. "I thought you might need it."

He crossed the room, got the blanket, and brought it back to her. He wrapped her in it, and she held it closed with her hands.

"Thank you." They stayed that way for a few seconds, looking into each other's eyes.

"Coffee smells ready," he said, standing up. "I'll get it."

He poured the coffee into two cups he got from his saddlebags and handed her one.

"Ooh, that feels good on my hands," she said, cradling the mug.

He sat back down in his chair next to her, holding his own mug.

"What are you going to do now?" she asked.

"Get some sleep," he said.

"Where?"

"Well, I thought here. You can sleep in that room, and I'll sleep in here."

"There's a cot in that room," she said. "What are you gonna sleep on?"

"I have my bedroll."

"On the floor?"

"Sure, why not?"

"It's so hard."

"Don't worry," he said. "I've slept on hard ground before."

She looked around.

"You don't even have a blanket."

"I've got my bedroll, like I said," Clint answered. "It'll do. More coffee?"

"Please."

He poured more for her, and for himself, sat back down, and handed it to her.

"You better turn in after this," he said. "More rest will do you good. Doc said he'll stop by tomorrow. Maybe he'll give us the go-ahead for you to ride out."

"I hope so," she said. "By being here, I'm not only risking my life, but yours, Doc's, and Amy's. I couldn't stand it if anything happened to any of you."

"You let me worry about that part," Clint said. "Staying alive is a specialty of mine."

TWENTY-SEVEN

The next morning Amy arrived early with breakfast.

"This is above and beyond the call of duty," Clint said, taking the tray from her at the door.

"I have to get back," she said. "I'll pick it up later. How's Mary?"

"She's good," he said. "Still asleep, but the smell of bacon might wake her. Thank you for this."

"Just doing my part."

"Believe me," Clint said, "you're doing more than your part."

She smiled, got in her buggy, and headed back to town. As Clint carried the tray in, Mary came from the other room, wrapped in a blanket.

"Who was that?" she asked.

"Amy, bringing breakfast," he said, putting the tray down on the table.

"Ooh, do I smell bacon?"

"You do."

They sat and she ate greedily.

"Your appetite looks good."

"I'm feeling a lot better," she said. "I bet I can travel."

"We'll let Doc decide that," he said, "but in any case, I'll go and look for a horse for you today."

"I'm really a good rider," she said. "If it wasn't for that cut cinch, I never would have fallen off my horse."

"I believe you," he said. "I'll get you something good."

"I'll trust you," she said, eating her last piece of bacon. "I have to go and get dressed."

"Did Amy bring you some other clothes?"

"I'm afraid not," she said. "She only brought me that one dress." She stood up. "I'm naked under this blanket."

"Naked?"

"Yes." She opened her arms. "See?"

She had a lovely body, which he'd only caught a glimpse of the day before. Now he saw two wonderfully round breasts, a dark pubic bush, full hips and thighs. All of which had been, until now, hidden beneath clothes and blankets.

Her nipples grew immediately hard and she closed the blanket, saying, "Still cold." She turned and ran into the other room, closing the door.

He wondered if he'd just been given an invitation. If he'd had nothing else to do, he might have accepted, but he decided to leave and head back to town. He took the tray with the plates and silverware with him, to save Amy the trouble.

Angela Locksley woke up the next morning feeling she had solved several problems at one time. Wes Tolbert would kill Clint Adams, getting him out of the way. Then he would take care of Mary Connelly. And finally, maybe she'd just have him kill her husband for her, so she wouldn't have to share her money with that parasite anymore. Once that was done, she'd get out of New Mexico, move to somewhere nice, like San Francisco.

But first things first.

Breakfast.

Angela thought it would be a simple thing to poison Eric at breakfast one day. Not today, though, since she was hungry.

Her husband came down and joined her at the table for breakfast.

"You've outdone yourself today, dear," he said, taking in the table filled with pancakes and bacon. "What's the occasion?"

"I woke in an extraordinarily good mood," she told him. Of course, he wouldn't know that because they slept in separate rooms.

"Well, I can use a meal like this," he said, seating himself.

"Why?" She sat across from him.

"I've got some hard decisions to make today."

"About that girl?" Angela asked. "And Clint Adams?"

"Yes, about them," he told her. "It's not easy deciding somebody's fate, you know. But you wouldn't know about that."

More and more, her husband was proving himself an idiot. She wondered how many of the decisions they made he thought were his alone.

TWENTY-EIGHT

It was a short walk to town, so he didn't bother saddling Eclipse.

"I told you I'd pick that up," Amy said when Clint entered the kitchen.

"You've got a lot of customers out there," he said, putting the tray aside. "I thought I'd save you the trouble."

"Well, thanks."

The cook gave Clint a dirty look. He was a young guy in a white apron, and from the way he looked at Amy, Clint knew why he was getting those looks.

"I'll see you later," he told Amy. "I'm going to see about getting Mary a horse."

"Are you leaving today?"

"She says she feels good," Clint said, "but it will be up to the doc when she leaves. I just want to be ready."

She accepted two plates from the cook then said to Clint, "Come back later and I'll have your lunch ready."

"Okay," he said. "Thanks."

He left the café, stopped a moment to take a look at

the street. He doubted the town drunk would be watching
him again, but the sheriff or Locksley might have sent
somebody more reliable. At the moment, however, he
didn't see anyone.

He headed for the livery stable.

Wes Tolbert left his hotel, thinking at that moment only
of breakfast. But there had also been a message waiting
for him at the front desk from Eric Locksley. Undoubt-
edly, Locksley had a job for him, but Tolbert never dis-
cussed business on an empty stomach.

He was walking on one side of the street, a particular
restaurant in mind as his goal, when he saw a man walking on the other side. He stopped and looked. He had no
doubt that the man was Clint Adams. It was in the way
he walked, and the way people on the street turned to
look at him.

Tolbert didn't move. If he did, he was sure he'd attract
the Gunsmith's attention. He stood where he was and
watched Clint Adams for as long as possible. By the time
Adams had faded from view, Tolbert was able to guess
that his destination was the livery stable.

With Adams gone, he was now free to move. He continued on to the restaurant, where he planned to have his
breakfast.

He could have braced Clint Adams there and then, but
just as he did not discuss business on an empty stomach,
he did not kill on an empty one either.

Eric Locksley sat behind his desk, waiting impatiently
for Wes Tolbert to show up. Tolbert was the man he'd

hired to do all of his dirty work for him. Getting rid of the Gunsmith and Mary Connelly certainly qualified as dirty work.

It never occurred to Locksley that this all could have been avoided if he had not taken up with Mary. What occurred to him was that this was all her fault, and he had to get rid of her. He thought he'd done that when he got the town to send her away on horseback, but she had come back. Now the tension he normally felt in his house between himself and his wife had become palpable. The only way to fix the situation this time was to get rid of Mary Connelly permanently. And with the Gunsmith championing her, he had to go as well.

Hence the call out to Wes Tolbert. Locksley checked the time. He knew the hired gunman would make him wait until after he had breakfast to appear. He had to put up with that because he feared Tolbert. But as long as he had the money to employ the man, Locksley was able to convince himself that he was in control.

Money meant control, and he had the money.

When Clint reached the livery, he had the liveryman show him a selection of horses, so he could pick one out for Mary.

"A man like you deserves better horses than these," the man told him. "I have other, more spirited mounts I can show you—"

"That's not necessary," Clint said. "I have a horse I'm very satisfied with. This horse is for someone else."

"Ah."

"A woman."

"Ahhh!"

Clint looked over the group in the corral, and his eye fell on a dappled gray mare about five years of age.

"I'll take that one."

"As you like," the man said. "When would you like it ready?"

"As soon as possible," Clint said. "I'll need a decent saddle, too."

"I got some inside," the man said. "Come on in and we can palaver over a jug."

"Palavering" over a price was the part of buying a horse Clint hated.

TWENTY-NINE

Clint was on his way back from the livery, having successfully purchased a horse and saddle that would suit Mary, when he saw a man walking on the other side of the street. He stopped short. He knew men like this from the way they walked, the way they wore a gun, the way people moved aside for them. He watched the man until he reached City Hall and went inside. Since he was obviously not a clerk, certainly not an alderman or a member of the town council—such men didn't wear a gun that way—he had to be going into that building for one reason, and one reason only.

Clint crossed the street, went through the City Hall door only moments behind the man. He was in time to see the gunman going up the stairs to the second floor.

Eric Locksley's floor.

He left the building and hurried back to Amy's small house, where he had left Mary and where, hopefully, she still was.

* * *

Mary was sitting in a chair out in front of the house.

"This is not a good idea," Clint said.

"It's musty inside."

"Well, somebody could see you out here. Come on, let's go inside."

She got up, and he picked up the chair and followed her inside.

"I got you a horse and a saddle," Clint said. "Was Doc here?"

"Not yet."

"Okay," Clint said, "I think after he comes, we should be on the move."

"Why? What happened?"

"I saw somebody in town." He told her about seeing the gunman. "He went upstairs, to Locksley's floor. What else is up there?"

"Nothing," she said. "He has the whole floor. That's where we used to meet . . . sometimes."

"Okay, so it looks like he's hiring a gun probably to take care of me."

"And me, I bet," she said.

They heard something outside, a buggy approaching.

"Amy?" she asked.

"Amy's busy," he said. "Maybe Doc. Go in the other room."

She went in and closed the door. Clint went to the front door, cracked it open, and looked out.

"It's okay," he called out. "It's Doc."

He went outside to meet the sawbones.

Doc got down from his buggy, carrying his bag.

"Good morning."

"Morning, Doc."

"How is she?"

"Better," Clint said. "She's showing quite an appetite."

The two men went into the house. Mary came out of the other room.

"Hey, Doc."

"You look better," he said. "Let me take a look at you. In there."

"Sure," she said, and went back into the room with him.

Clint made a pot of coffee while he waited for them. He heard the sounds of voices droning on behind the closed door. When they came out, he was sitting at the table, drinking coffee.

"How's she doing?" Clint asked.

"She's good," Doc said.

"Can she ride?"

"I'd still give it a couple of days."

"We may not have a couple of days."

"She told me about the gunman you saw," Doc said. Mary poured him a cup of coffee and handed it to him. She didn't take one for herself.

"Describe him," Doc said.

"Tall, black clothes, carries the right shoulder lower than the left—"

"Stop," Doc said. "That's Wes Tolbert."

"You know him?"

"I've taken a bullet or two out of him," Doc said. "He's good."

"Is he for hire?"

Doc nodded.

"That's what he does. He kills for money."

"Great."

"You're going to have to go up against him, Clint," Doc said. "If he's been hired, he won't quit. You can't just leave town. He'll track you. Then he'll kill you. And once you're dead, Mary."

"Okay, Doc," Clint said. "I get it."

Doc turned and looked at Mary.

"Looks like the time to just leave town is over."

"Thanks for everything, Doc," she said.

Mathis nodded and Clint walked him out.

"Doc, you think Tolbert will come after you?"

"He will if Locksley tells him to," Mathis said. "But this town needs a doctor, so I think I'm safe."

"Okay," Clint said.

Doc got into his buggy.

"I've got some other stops to make, and then I'll be in town. Give me a few hours."

"For what?"

"I want to be available when you take on Tolbert," Mathis said. "I might have to take a bullet or two out of you."

"Or him," Clint said.

"I'm hoping it won't go either of those ways, Clint," Doc Mathis said.

He turned his buggy and headed back to town. Clint watched until he was gone, then went back into the house.

THIRTY

When Tolbert walked into Locksley's office, the man said, "Have a seat."

Tolbert walked slowly to a chair and sat in it.

"How was breakfast?" Locksley asked.

"Ham and eggs," Tolbert said. "Real nice biscuits. It was good."

"Good, I'm glad you're well fed," Locksley said. "I know how you hate to kill on an empty stomach."

"Am I gonna be killin' somebody?"

"A man and a woman," Locksley said. "Have you got a problem with killing a woman?"

"Not if the money's right."

"Don't worry, the money will be right. The woman is Mary Connelly. You know her?"

"I thought you knew her pretty well."

"Never mind that," Locksley said. "You're going to kill her."

"I thought you got rid of her."

"She came back, and brought a man with her," Locksley said. "I want them both killed."

"You care how?"

"That's your job."

"Okay, then. The only thing we have to talk about is money."

"I'll pay you twice your normal fee."

Tolbert's eyebrows shot up.

"Why so generous?" he asked. "I usually have to fight for my usual fee."

"The man," Locksley said. "He's a special case."

"What's so special about him?"

"His name is Clint Adams."

Tolbert had already heard that from Angela Locksley, but he acted surprised.

"The Gunsmith," he said. "You know, I think I saw him on the street."

"How would you know?" Locksley asked. "Have you ever met him?"

"No, but people stepped aside for him," Locksley said. "Usually, the folks in this town only do that for me."

"Yeah," Locksley said, "he's a killer, like you. Can you do it? Can you kill the Gunsmith?"

"I can," Locksley said, "but like you said, he's a special case."

"What's that mean?"

"Triple my usual fee."

Locksley opened a drawer, took out a thick brown envelope, and tossed it to Tolbert, who caught it, hefted it.

"You knew I'd ask for triple," he said. "Could I have gotten more?"

"Don't be greedy, Wes," Locksley said. "Just get the job done. I've paid you in advance."

Tolbert stood up, hefted the envelope.

"Okay. I'll get it done."

"Today?" Locksley asked.

"My earliest opportunity."

"What's that mean?"

Tolbert walked to the door, turned with his hand on the doorknob.

"It means as soon as the time is right, Mr. Locksley," he said. "The situation has to be right."

"Okay, okay," Locksley said, "just get it done."

"Oh, I'll get it done," Tolbert said. He hefted the envelope again. "I'll get it done."

As he left, Locksley sat back in his chair. Once Tolbert had killed Adams, and Mary, then Locksley would be free to kill Tolbert.

Wouldn't that surprise Angela?

THIRTY-ONE

Clint sat with Mary in the house.

"What are we going to do?" she asked. "It seems like Eric definitely wants us dead. Or Angela does."

"Yeah," Clint said, "it looks like just leaving town isn't an option anymore."

"Can't we sneak out?"

"If Doc is right about Tolbert, he'll track us," Clint said.

"Then what can we do?"

"I'll have to go and find him," Clint said, "and get it over with."

"Kill him?"

"Talk him out of wanting to kill us," Clint said.

"Do you think you can?" she asked.

"I can try," Clint said. "It'll depend on two things."

"Like what?"

"How much he's getting paid," Clint said, "and how badly he wants to be the man who kills the Gunsmith."

"How many men have tried already?" she asked.

"Over the years," he said, "too many to count."

Angela opened her front door and was startled to see Wes Tolbert standing there.

"What the hell are you doing here?" she demanded.

"Invite me in before somebody sees me."

"Oh!" She stepped back to let him in, then looked around before closing the door. In the foyer she turned to face him. "Why are you here?"

"I just came from a meeting with your husband," he said. "He wants me to kill Adams and the girl."

"Well, so do I," she said. "Do it!"

"He paid me in advance."

"If you remember," she said, "I gave you something in advance as well."

"And that was real nice," Tolbert said. "But he gave me money. A lot of money."

"Wes," she said, "I thought we had something." She put her hands on his chest.

"We do, Angela," Tolbert said. "We both have a love of money—yours and your husband's."

She dropped her hands.

"So you want to be paid now?"

"Yes, please."

"And when will you get the job done?" she asked.

"As soon as possible."

"Very well," she said. "Wait here."

He knew he could follow her. She was probably going to a safe to get the money out. He could empty the entire safe.

But that could all wait until later. Better to get paid for the job, and get the job done. Then he could worry about Mr. and Mrs. Locksley.

She came back with an envelope similar to the one her husband had given him, also bulging.

"This ought to be enough," she said, handing it to him.

He hefted it and said, "Feels like it."

"So go and do it," she said, folding her arms beneath her breasts. "I'll be waiting here when you get back."

"Waiting for me?" he asked. "Or for your husband?"

"What do you think?" she asked.

He nodded, smiled, and turned toward the door.

"And Wes?"

"Yeah?"

"If a stray bullet happened to find my husband . . ."

He nodded again, and left.

THIRTY-TWO

Clint had a dilemma.

If he went into town to find Tolbert, leaving Mary alone, then Tolbert might find Mary. It probably didn't matter to the gunman which of them he killed first. He could have left Mary a gun, but even with a weapon, she'd probably be no match for Tolbert.

"Come on," he said.

"Where?"

"I've got to put you somewhere else safe," he said, "before I go to . . . talk to Tolbert."

"But where?"

"That's a good question."

"Why can't I stay here?"

"I'll tell you on the way."

They went outside, and he explained it to her while he saddled Eclipse.

"I *can* handle a gun, you know," she told him when he was finished.

"Not against this man," Clint said. "That'll be my job."

With Eclipse saddled, Clint lifted Mary into the saddle.

"I've never been on a horse this big."

"The Darley Arabians are built bigger, thicker, pretty much for stamina."

He walked them back to town, but instead of going down the main street, he took them behind the buildings, sticking to alleys. Finally, they reached Doc's office.

"Back here?" she asked.

"I don't think they'd look here again," Clint said.

He helped her down from the horse, then took a good look at the street before he let her go up the stairs ahead of him.

"Didn't expect to see you again so soon," Doc said as he let them in.

Clint explained the situation to Doc, who understood.

"It's probably a good idea to bring her back here, then," he said. "You figure to resolve this today?"

"I hope so," Clint said. "I'm going to talk to everyone involved and see what I can do."

"And if talking doesn't work?"

"I think we know how it will go, then."

"Don't forget Locksley's got the sheriff in his pocket," Doc said. "If you kill his gunman, Crabtree might try to stick you in a cell."

"I figured," Clint said. "That's why I'm going to talk to him first."

Sheriff Crabtree turned from the stove as his door opened and Clint walked in. He looked surprised, turned the rest of the way, coffeepot in his hand.

"Sure, I'll have a cup," Clint said. "Thanks."

Crabtree looked at the pot as if he just realized he was holding it. He shook his head, poured two cups, set one on the desk for Clint, then sat down.

"What can I do for you, Adams?"

Clint sat down, ignored the coffee.

"Locksley's hired a gun," Clint said, "but you probably know that."

"Why would I?"

Clint ignored the question.

"His name's Wes Tolbert. You know him?"

"I know Tolbert," Crabtree said. "He's got a big rep. Wouldn't want him after me."

"Well, I guess he's after me," Clint said, "and then the girl."

"Whataya want from me?" the lawman asked. "You got proof?"

"I'm just telling you," Clint said, "so if I end up killing Tolbert, you'll know why."

"You kill a man in this town and I'll have to arrest you."

"If I was you, I wouldn't want to try that, Sheriff," Clint said.

Sheriff Crabtree swallowed hard. "Are you threatening me?"

"I'm just advising you," Clint said. "If you're not going to do your job, don't get in my way. If Tolbert comes for me, I'll defend myself."

"That sounds fair."

"And then I'll go after whoever hired him."

"And you think that's Mr. Locksley?"

"I do."

Sheriff Crabtree swallowed again before speaking, and it seemed to be even more difficult this time. He sipped his coffee to wet his lips.

"I—I c-can't let you go after our leading citizen, Adams."

Clint stood up.

"You can't stop me either, Crabtree," he said. "Just remember what I told you."

The sheriff didn't stand as Clint walked to the door and went out. Crabtree let out a long breath. He wasn't getting paid enough to cross the Gunsmith. He took a bottle of whiskey from his desk drawer and poured a generous amount into his coffee.

He was going to have to get drunk enough to decide who scared him more—the Gunsmith, or Wes Tolbert working for Eric Locksley.

Clint stopped in front of the sheriff's office, figuring his next move. Wes Tolbert had been hired to kill him, of that he was sure. And he'd seen the man going into City Hall. But what if he was working for Mrs. Locksley, not Mr.? Or if he was working for Eric Locksley, Angela might be able to talk some sense into her husband.

That is, if Clint was able to talk some sense into Angela Locksley.

THIRTY-THREE

Clint approached the Locksley house, assuming—and hoping—that the man of the house was in his office. Angela Locksley opened the door in response to his knock, and he was surprised when she smiled.

"Mr. Adams. What an unexpected pleasure. Come in, please."

Clint entered the house warily, in case she had a man with a gun behind the door.

"Come into the living room and I'll give you a drink," she said, leading the way. "I assume it's not too early for a man like you?"

"A man like me?" he asked.

"Well, yes," she said. "A man who faces death every day? I suspect it's never too early for you to have a drink. Am I wrong?"

"Actually," he said, "probably not."

"Good," she said, "then you'll have a glass of sherry?"

"I thought you said a drink."

"Very well," she said. "Whiskey it is."

She poured a whiskey for him, and then one for herself. She was wearing a heavy robe that hung to her ankles, belted tightly at the waist. As she approached him and handed him his glass, he could smell the scent she was wearing, slightly fruity but heady.

"Here's to dangerous living," she said.

"That's not a toast I can drink to."

"Come up with another one, then," she said.

"Here's to second chances."

"I'll drink to that," she said, and they did. Then she said, "Whose second chances are we talking about?"

"Let's discuss yours."

"Mine?" she asked. "Why do I need a second chance?"

"Second chances to do the right thing."

"And what would the right thing be?"

"Calling off Wes Tolbert."

She paused with her glass to her lips, then completed the motion before asking, "And should I know who that is?"

"Why not?" Clint asked. "Everyone else in town knows he's a killer."

"Oh, that man," she said. "What is it you think I should call him off of?"

"I know he's been hired to kill me, and Mary," Clint said. "He's either working for you, or for your husband. So you can call him off, or convince your husband to call him off."

"Are you afraid of this man?"

"No," Clint said, "I just don't want to have to kill anyone. I only came to this town to get an injured woman some treatment. I didn't expect I'd have to end up killing someone."

"Isn't that something you're used to by now?"

"You never get used to killing," he said. "If you do, there's something wrong with you inside."

"Odd words coming from a killer."

"I have little interest in your opinion of me, Mrs. Locksley," he said. "If you didn't hire Tolbert, then your husband did. I'll go and talk to him."

"Talk to him, then," she said. "What's done is done. That girl is not going to get to leave this town alive again."

"It's a shame you feel that way," he said, putting his glass down. "She's under my protection, and anyone who tries to harm her is going to have to answer to me. That includes you, your husband, and your hired gun."

"I'll be very interested to see how this all turns out, Mr. Adams," she said. "Very interested."

"Badly, Mrs. Locksley," he assured her. "It's going to turn out badly for everyone involved."

THIRTY-FOUR

Clint left the house, convinced that Angela Locksley knew everything there was to know about Wes Tolbert. He still wasn't sure who was paying the man, though. Everyone in town seemed to think she wore the pants in her family, but it was possible that when Locksley was out of the house, he made his own decisions.

He walked back to town, wondering if he'd encounter Wes Tolbert before he could get to Eric Locksley. And, of course, the sheriff could already be there, looking for orders. Or turning in his badge. It didn't seem likely that Sheriff Crabtree would have the courage to face either Tolbert or Clint. He may have gone as far in his job as he could.

Clint made it to City Hall without seeing either Tolbert or Crabtree. He entered and went directly to the second floor. As he entered the office, Gina Hopewell looked up at him with a ready smile, but it fell when she saw him.

"You!" she said accusingly. "You were supposed to come and see me."

"I'm sorry," he said, "I've been very busy, Gina. Is your boss in?"

"He is, but you don't have an appointment," she said, not at all mollified.

"I'm sorry," he said. "I hope this doesn't get you in trouble, but I have to go in and see him."

"You can't—" she started, but she saw immediately that she wasn't going to be able to stop him.

Clint burst into the man's office, slamming the door open, trying to set the tone of the meeting to his benefit right away.

Locksley looked up from his desk with a quick jerk of his head, then his eyes widened when he saw Clint.

"I'm sorry, Mrs. Lock—" Gina started to say, but Clint slammed the door in her face.

"What the hell do you think you're doing?" Locksley demanded.

"You've got a hired gun on your payroll," Clint said. "Wes Tolbert—"

"I have no such th—"

"I've seen him here."

"I don't even know the man!"

"We're beyond that, Locksley," Clint said. "There's no point in lying. Everybody in town knows that Wes Tolbert is a gunman."

"That may be," Locksley said, "but that doesn't mean I hired him."

"If you didn't, then your wife did."

"My wife?" Locksley said. "You're crazy."

"I'll tell you what I'm going to do, Locksley," Clint said. "If you don't call him off, just before I kill him, I'm going to make him tell me who hired him. If I find out it was you, I'll be back. And if it was your wife, she'll be seeing me."

"You wouldn't kill a woman."

"I'll kill anyone who tries to kill me," Clint said. "Or don't you know my reputation?"

This was one time Clint was trying to trade on the fact that reputations are overblown.

"If you come near me or my wife, I'll have the law on you!" Locksley blustered as Clint headed for the door.

"You better talk to your sheriff," Clint said. "I think he might be ready for a career change. I wouldn't depend very much on him, if I was you."

Clint went out the door. Gina wasn't at her desk. He figured she didn't want to see him when he left, but he couldn't worry too much about that. There was too much else to think about.

THIRTY-FIVE

Talking had done no good.

Clint left City Hall knowing he was going to have to deal with Wes Tolbert. What he didn't know was whether or not Tolbert would come right at him, or if he'd come with or without help.

If Clint could get some background information on the gunman, it would be real helpful to him. But who would have that kind of information? Normally, he'd try the local law, but Crabtree would be no help at all. And most of the people were afraid of the power Eric Locksley wielded.

He started off down the street, still trying to think of who in town could be helpful, when he spotted the Dry Wash Saloon. He remembered the bartender named Max. If anyone could be helpful, it would probably be him.

He crossed the street and entered the saloon. Max was behind the bar, and there were some scattered customers drinking by themselves, but nobody leaning on the bar.

Clint approached the bar and Max came to meet him.

"Cold beer?" Max asked.

"Sounds good."

Max brought him the beer.

"What's the word around town, Max?" he asked.

"About what?"

"I think you know," Clint said. "About me, and Mary Connelly."

"The word I hear is you're both as good as dead."

"Because of Wes Tolbert?"

"You know him?"

"Never heard of him before I came here," Clint said. "Now I'm hearing all about him. What do you know?"

"Tolbert's not from here originally, but he's been here about five years. Locksley brought him in for a job and he stayed. Been makin' a name for himself ever since."

"By killing people?"

"You got it."

"Has he ever been arrested?"

"Not in this town, or this country," Max said. "Not with Locksley backin' him."

"I see."

"That's what you call general information," Max said.

"You got some private information that nobody else has?" Clint asked.

"I got somethin'."

Clint went into his pocket for some money.

"Naw, naw," Max said, "I ain't tryin' to hold you up for money. Fact is, if you can get rid of Tolbert and the Locksleys, that'd be all the payment I need."

"Okay, then," Clint said. "What have you got?"

Max looked around, leaned on the bar, and lowered his voice.

"Word I hear is that while Locksley was rollin' around in his office with Mary Connelly, his wife was rollin' around in the hay with Tolbert."

"What?"

"That's what I hear." Mac straightened up.

"I was wondering who had hired Tolbert, the husband or the wife," Clint said.

"Well," Max said, "maybe the husband paid him money, and the wife is givin' him somethin' else."

"Do you know anything about his work?" Clint asked.

"Whataya wanna know?" Max asked.

"Does he work alone?"

"He gets help when he needs it," Max said. "Depends on what the job calls for."

"Well, it calls for him to kill me," Clint said. "What I want to know is, is he going to come straight at me on the street? Or do I have to worry about being bushwhacked?"

"I've seen Tolbert gun men down in the street," Max said, "but that don't mean he ain't bushwhacked one or two in his day. I wouldn't put it past him."

"That's what I wanted to know," Clint said.

"I'd watch my back if I was you," Max said, "but if Tolbert's lookin' to pad his reputation, he'll come right at you."

"Is he fast?"

"He's fast," Max said, "and he's cool under pressure. He ain't gonna make no mistakes."

Clint nodded. In the past he'd always been able to count on men making a mistake. On occasion he had faced a cool one, and those were the ones who turned out to be the most dangerous.

"I'd say he's a dangerous man," Max said, as if reading Clint's mind.

"I got that," Clint said. He finished his beer, pushed the empty mug across the bar. "Thanks for the information, Max."

"Good luck to you, Mr. Adams," Max said. "I got my fingers crossed for you."

As Clint turned to leave, Max asked, "If it turns out you two face each other in the street, you mind if I come out and watch?"

"Why not?" Clint asked. "Everybody else will."

THIRTY-SIX

Tolbert sat in the window of his hotel room, watching the main street. He saw Clint Adams visit the sheriff, then disappear for a while before reappearing and entering City Hall to see Eric Locksley. In between he would have been collecting as much information as possible on Wes Tolbert.

But that didn't matter. Let Adams collect as much knowledge as he could. It was all in Tolbert's gun, and in his plans. He had to be sure that when it was all over, he had Angela and all the Locksley money. He was going to need some backup before he faced Clint Adams, to be on the safe side.

Let Adams sweat for a day or so.

Clint got back to Doc's without running up against Wes Tolbert.

"Oh, God," Mary said as he walked in. She hugged him. "I was so worried."

"I didn't hear any shooting," Doc Mathis said.

"No shooting, just a lot of talking," Clint said.

"Who'd you talk to?"

"Everybody," Clint said. "I ended up gabbing with Max over at the Dry Wash."

"Max knows everything about everybody in town," Mathis said.

"Well, he gave me some knowledge about Wes Tolbert, both generally known and not so generally known."

"Like what?"

"Like Tolbert and Mrs. Locksley."

"Well," Mary said, "good for her."

"But maybe not so good for us," Clint said. "It's bad enough when a man is doing a job for money, but if he's doing it for love . . ."

"Love?" Mary asked. "Angela? I don't think so. Sex, maybe, but there also has to be something else in it for her."

"Like her husband's money?" Clint asked.

"The money's already hers," Doc said. "I think she's more interested in getting her husband's power. She can't have complete control over the town until he dies."

"And with all the bullets that might be flying around," Clint said, "who's to say one won't hit Locksley?"

THIRTY-SEVEN

Wes Tolbert waited at a back table in the Dry Wash Saloon with a bottle of whiskey and three glasses. He also had a beer in front of him. None of the whiskey glasses would be used until his friends arrived.

A saloon girl came over and asked, "Another beer, Wes?"

"Sure, Liz. Bring me a nice cold one."

"What about the whiskey?" she asked. "You gonna drink it?"

"I will, real soon."

Liz turned and walked away. Beyond her, Tolbert saw the batwings open. Dan Cutter and Billy Aaron walked in. Cutter looked around, spotted him, and nudged Aaron. They crossed the floor, pushing two men out of the way.

"Hey, Wes," Cutter said.

"Dan," Tolbert said. "Have a seat."

The two men sat.

"Billy," Tolbert said. "Whiskey?"

"Don't mind if I do."

Tolbert poured the three glasses full and they all drank. Nobody spoke until he filled them again.

"What's this all about, Wes?" Cutter asked. "You come across a job you need our help fer?"

"I did," Tolbert said.

"That don't happen much," Aaron said. "You can pretty much handle anybody."

"I still can," Tolbert said. "I'm just looking for a little insurance."

"The kind we get paid for?" Cutter asked.

"That's right, Dan," Tolbert said, "the kind you get paid for."

"How much?" Aaron asked.

"We'll get to that later," Tolbert said. "First, you boys should know who I'm going up against."

"And who's that?" Cutter asked.

"Clint Adams," Tolbert said, and then just in case they didn't get it, he added, "The Gunsmith."

Cutter stared at Tolbert for a few moments, then grabbed the bottle and poured three glasses again.

"This job's gonna pay good," he said, clinking glasses with Billy Aaron.

"What do we gotta do?" Aaron asked.

"For now," Tolbert said, "all you've got to do is listen . . ."

It was getting late—dusk—and Locksley hadn't heard any shots yet. He'd been waiting, even when Gina came in to say good night.

"Are you going home, sir?"

"Soon, Gina," he'd said. "You go ahead."

Locksley didn't want to be in the street when the shooting started. Now it was getting dark. Would Tolbert try anything in the dark? Probably not.

Time to go home, to the little woman.

Usually, when there was shooting in town, she could hear it from the house. So far, she hadn't heard a thing. Looked as if Tolbert was going to let the day go without getting the job done. Maybe he was planning it for the next.

She went to the kitchen to get supper ready. She liked cooking, and she liked eating, she just didn't like cooking for and eating with her husband. Maybe it would only be a day or two more, and then she'd be on her own. Maybe she would even have her son come back from the East and it would be the two of them for a while.

When it was all over, the only problem would be getting rid of Wes Tolbert.

THIRTY-EIGHT

Doc Mathis once again agreed to allow Clint and Mary to spend the night.

"And this time," he added, "I'll go and get the food. I don't want Tolbert spotting you in the street and shooting you while you're carrying my steak."

"Thanks, Doc," Clint said.

After Doc left to pick up supper, Clint watched Mary make the beds up again for them. After she finished hers, she sat on it and stared at him.

"I'm sorry about all this," she said.

"It's not your fault."

"Sure it is," she said. "If I hadn't got involved with Eric, he wouldn't have had to drive me out of town. I wouldn't've fallen off my horse, and you wouldn't've found me and brought me here. And you wouldn't have to face Tolbert."

"Believe me, Mary," Clint said, "Tolbert won't be a problem."

"How can you be so sure?" she asked. "Are you that confident?"

"I'm very confident of my ability with a gun," he said. "I also came to terms long ago with the fact that I'll probably die by a bullet. But I'm also pretty sure I'll feel the when and where, and this isn't it."

"Wow," she said. "I wish I knew when and where I was gonna die."

"I didn't say I knew it," he said "I said I'd feel it."

"And you don't feel it now?"

"No."

"What if Tolbert doesn't come for you alone?" she asked.

"Well, that'll increase the odds that he'll survive instead of me," he explained, "but I've faced superior odds before."

"You should have help."

"The only people who have been helping have been Doc and Amy, and neither of them is good with a gun," Clint said.

"I can shoot."

"When the time comes," he said, "the best thing the three of you can do is stay out of harm's way. If I have to worry about you, that's when I could get killed."

"I understand."

"Don't worry," he told her. "It'll all be over soon."

Cutter and Aaron listened intently while Wes Tolbert told them their job. When he was done, he poured the last of the whiskey into their glasses.

"Are you sure that's all you want us to do?" Cutter asked.

"Hey," Aaron said, "don't change his mind. I'd rather do this than face Clint Adams in the street. That's up to Tolbert."

"This is the way I want to do it," Tolbert said. "When this is over, I'm going to end up with a reputation, and with money."

"And what are we gonna end up with?" Cutter asked.

"A lot of money," Tolbert said, "and maybe the run of the town. How would you like that? Anything in town you want."

"What about the law?" Aaron asked.

"The sheriff around here won't be a problem," Tolbert said. "And the town's already used to bein' run roughshod over."

Tolbert waved Liz over, and while the saloon had become a lot busier while they'd been there, she saw him and came right over.

"Honey, can you bring me and my friends another bottle?"

"Sure thing, Wes."

"And three beers," Cutter said.

"Yeah," Tolbert said, "three beers."

"Comin' up."

Liz was a cute blonde, and when she turned and walked away, they watched her butt twitch, like she was winking at them.

"When you say we can have anythin' in town we want," Aaron said, "you mean anythin'?"

"Anythin'," Tolbert said.

"What about whoever's payin' you?" Aaron asked.

"He's the one's been runnin' this town up to now," Tolbert said, "and he's the one you and Dan here are gonna take care of. After that, it's all ours."

"You got this all figured out?" Cutter asked.

"I got it all figured out, boys," Tolbert said. "And all I got to do to make it happen is kill the Gunsmith."

THIRTY-NINE

There was a heavy knock on Doc's door early the next morning, like the knock of an anxious man. Doc answered, found that it was Amy kicking the door with her foot because her hands were full.

"Breakfast," she announced, entering.

Clint came out of the spare room buttoning his shirt.

"I don't know that I've ever eaten this well," he commented. "Or had service this good."

"Don't get too used to it," she said, setting the tray down. "I can't do it every day."

"Hopefully," Clint said, "we're close to the end."

Mary came out from the other room and smiled at Amy.

"I thought I smelled bacon."

"Plenty of it," Amy said. "Enjoy. I got to get back to the café."

Mathis walked her to the door, closed and locked it behind her.

"Jesus," he said, "I thought it was trouble when she kicked that door."

"Trouble wouldn't have knocked," Clint told him. "Trouble kicks the door in."

But as they sat down to eat, he knew that trouble was looming. Maybe there was something he could do that day to head it off.

Locksley had gotten into a shouting match the night before with his wife. She wanted something done, kept yelling "Now!" so he rose early the next morning and went to his office without breakfast.

So because he was early, he was surprised when Sheriff Crabtree walked in.

"What do you want this early?" he demanded.

Crabtree took the star off his chest and dropped it on Locksley's desk.

"Get yourself another sheriff," Crabtree said.

"What's the matter with you?"

"I think you know," the man said. "Things are about to explode in this town, and I don't want no part of it."

"You're a coward!"

"You're probably right," Crabtree said.

"Don't come crawling to me when it's all over and think you'll get this back."

"That would take a lot of crawling, since I'm leavin' town right now. Good luck."

Crabtree left and Locksley picked up the badge and fingered it. He made a quick decision, stood up, and left the office. He was going to find Wes Tolbert and pin the badge on him before he made his move on Clint Adams.

* * *

Wes Tolbert was coming out of his hotel when he saw Locksley striding purposefully toward him.

"Glad I caught you," the man said. "Here."

"What's this?" He looked down at the badge Locksley had jammed into his hand.

"You're the new sheriff."

"What happened to Crabtree?"

"He retired."

Tolbert looked down at the badge then back at his boss.

"This might make things a little easier."

"That's what I was thinking," Locksley said. "Now whatever you do, you can do in an official capacity."

Tolbert pinned the badge onto his shirt.

"How do I look?"

"Like a man with a job to do," Locksley said, "so do it!"

"Where are you gonna be today?" Tolbert asked.

"In my office," Locksley said. "Why?"

"I'm thinking today's the day."

"Well then," Locksley said, "I'll definitely be in my office."

He turned and headed back to his office. He wanted to be off the street when the shooting started.

The badge felt odd on Tolbert's chest. He'd never even thought about being on this side of the badge.

He turned as his two men, Cutter and Aaron, came out of the hotel.

"What the hell is that on your chest?" Cutter asked.

"I told you yesterday you wouldn't have to worry about

the law," Tolbert said. "Now I'm damn sure of it. The sheriff retired and left town."

"So you're the new sheriff?" Aaron asked.

"That's right. And another thing. Locksley is gonna be in his office all day, so there's no chance you'll have to go looking for him."

"So when do we do this?" Cutter asked.

"Stay available," Tolbert said.

"Like where?" Aaron asked.

"Like right there." Tolbert pointed to two wooden chairs in front of the hotel.

"What do we do while we wait?"

"Whittle," Locksley suggested.

FORTY

Clint was on the street when ex-Sheriff Crabtree went riding by. He noticed the man was not wearing his badge.

"Sheriff!"

Crabtree turned, saw Clint, and reined in. Clint stepped into the street.

"Not the sheriff anymore, Adams," Crabtree said.

"Where are you headed?"

"Away from here," the ex-lawman said, "before the lead starts flyin'. I don't aim to get between you and Wes Tolbert."

"So if you're not the law, who is?"

"I don't know," Crabtree said, "but knowing Locksley, I can guess who he'd pin the badge on."

"Tolbert?"

Crabtree nodded. "Good luck to you," he said, and urged his horse forward.

Clint watched the man ride out of town, wondering if Locksley had indeed pinned the badge on Tolbert, and what that would mean in the near—very near—future.

                              *   *   *

The Dry Wash was Wes Tolbert's saloon of choice, so he
decided to pull a wooden chair up in front and wait for
Clint Adams to put in an appearance.

Angela Locksley wondered if she should get dressed and
go to town to watch the action. She could feel it in the air
that today was the day. Her husband had run out early,
and she hadn't seen Wes Tolbert since the day before. In
the end she decided to take the walk, and to dress for the
occasion with trousers, a cotton shirt, boots, and a
new hat.

Locksley watched the street from his window. From there
he could see the hotel and the saloon, noticed the men
seated in front of both locations. He wondered if the two
men in front of the hotel were working for Tolbert.
    This would be a good vantage point to watch the action
from. He folded his arms and waited.

Clint walked down the main street, spotted the glint of
metal on the chest of Wes Tolbert, seated in front of the
Dry Wash Saloon. He crossed the street and approached
the new lawman.
    "I see congratulations are in order," he said.
    "Thanks," Tolbert said. "My first time on this side of
the badge."
    "How does it feel?"
    Tolbert thought a moment, then said, "Odd."
    "In the market for deputies?"
    "Why?" Tolbert asked. "You looking for a job?"

"My badge-wearing days are well behind me," Clint said. "No, I was just wondering."

"I haven't been in the job long enough to know yet if I'll need deputies."

"What's your first bit of business going to be?" Clint asked. "To drive me out of town?"

"Naw," Tolbert said, "you can stay. The place would be boring without you, wouldn't it?"

"How's your boss feel about that?"

"Mr. Locksley would like me to do the job the best way I know how."

"That sure doesn't sound like the same man I met," Clint said.

"He's different men to different people," Tolbert said.

"That I can believe," Clint said, "and from what I hear, nobody likes whoever he is to them."

Tolbert didn't comment on that.

"When are you leaving town?"

"Left alone," Clint said, "I think I'd be leaving tomorrow."

"With the girl?"

"That's right," Clint said, "but I think both you and I know I'm not going to be left alone, right?"

"I'm the law now, Adams," Tolbert said. "If anybody bothers you, you just let me know."

"Yeah," Clint said, "I'll do that."

Clint backed away a few steps before turning his back and walking away.

Eric Locksley watched from his window as Clint Adams stopped to talk with new Sheriff Tolbert. He expected the encounter to erupt into gunfire, but he was disappointed—especially when Clint Adams turned his back and walked away. That was the perfect opportunity for Tolbert to finish the job.

What the hell was he thinking?

As Clint walked away from the Dry Wash and Sheriff Tolbert, he passed the hotel. Sitting in front were two men. One of them took great pains to look away from him, while the other looked straight at him. Clint touched the brim of his hat as he walked by. He had no doubt that these two were with Tolbert. Obviously, the man had made his decision, decided that he needed backup.

Clint figured he now knew what he was up against.

Aaron asked, "Why are you lookin' at him?"

"The man's a legend, Billy," Cutter said. "How many times you get to see an actual legend?"

"You ask me," Aaron said, "this is one time too many."

Tolbert could have back shot Clint Adams as he was walking away, but how would he manage to make that sound official?

No, he let him walk away, but it wouldn't be long now. Not long at all.

FORTY-ONE

Clint wasn't sure just how to prod this along. Apparently marching right up to Tolbert wasn't going to work. The man wasn't going to make a move until he was ready.

He walked back to Doc Mathis's place, in time to see the doc climbing aboard his buggy.

"What's going on?" he asked.

"I've got a woman going into labor," Mathis said. "I've got to go to her."

"What about Mary?"

"I figured she'd be all right here alone."

"I'd rather you take her with you, Doc," Clint said. "Press her into service as a nurse. Maybe by the time you both get back, this'll all be over."

"Maybe you've got a point." He got down from the buggy. "I'll go up and get her. Did you see Tolbert?"

"I did," Clint said. "He's not ready to make a move yet."

"How will you get him to be ready?"

"Just make myself available, I guess."

"Well, be careful. Sure you don't want some help?"

"I'd love some help," Clint said. "Can you tell me where to get it?"

"I've got a gun—"

"No, Doc," Clint said. "I need you and Mary to be out of town."

"Okay."

Doc went up the stairs, came down a few moments later with Mary. Clint helped her into the buggy.

"Clint, are you sure I can't sta—"

"This is the best way, Mary," Clint said. "Doc, don't go down the main street. That might be too much temptation for Tolbert and his men."

"His men?" Doc asked.

"Yeah, it looks like he brought in two men to back him up."

"Oh, God, two men?" Mary asked. "Three against one?"

"Those odds are not as bad as they might have been," Clint said.

"Clint," she said, "I—"

"Get going, Doc," Clint said. "Keep her away from town until dark."

"It'll probably take me that long to deliver the child," Doc said. "We'll see you later, Clint—I hope."

"I hope so, too."

Impulsively, Mary leaned over and kissed Clint on the corner of the mouth.

After Doc and Mary drove away, Clint turned and went back to the main street. He considered going over to the Dry Wash. With Tolbert sitting in front of the place, it would make sure he knew where Clint was when the time came. But before Clint could head that way, he saw someone walking down the street who was familiar to him. As she walked, men and women stepped aside for her—probably out of deference to her husband.

Clint crossed the street and stepped in front of her. She stopped abruptly.

"Mr. Adams," she said. "Hello."

"Mrs. Locksley," he said. "Where are you heading?"

"Why, to see my husband."

"At work?" he asked. "Wouldn't that upset him, being interrupted?"

"I'm afraid we had a quarrel this morning," she said. "I want to mend fences before he comes home tonight."

"I see," he said. "Well, let me walk you there."

"Oh, that won't be—"

"I wouldn't hear of letting you walk there alone," Clint said. "There are a couple of strange men in town, and you'll have to walk right past them. I'll make sure they don't bother you."

He extended his arm.

"All right," she said, linking her arm in his. "Let's go."

FORTY-TWO

First, they had to walk past Tolbert's two men, seated across the street in front of the saloon. This time both men stared openly at Angela Locksley.

Next they passed Tolbert. The new sheriff didn't move when he saw them.

"Looks like somebody got a new job," Clint said to her.

"What? Oh," she said, peering across at Tolbert. "Is that a badge?"

"Seems your husband appointed him this morning."

"What happened to Crabtree?"

"Left town," Clint said. "I saw him leave."

Finally, on their own side of the street, they reached City Hall. Clint saw Locksley standing in the window above before he could duck out of sight.

"You might as well join your husband, Angela," Clint said. "I think he has a good vantage point up there."

"Good luck, Mr. Adams," she said. "You should never have come here to Heathstead."

"Believe me, Mrs. Locksley," he said. "If I had known, I wouldn't have."

He opened the door for her, closed it after she had gone in. He saw a small saloon just across the street, decided to stop inside there instead of the Dry Wash for a drink.

Tolbert saw Clint walk across the street to the Black Jack Saloon, decided it was time. He waved at Cutter and Aaron, giving them the signal. They already had instructions to make sure Mrs. Locksley came to no harm, if she happened to be around at the time. She was, after all, his route to the money.

"That's it," Cutter said. "Time to go."

"You sure?"

"That's the signal," Cutter said, "and everybody seems to be in place."

"Well . . . okay."

They stood up, walked down the street, and then across until they were in front of City Hall. Aaron opened the door, and they went inside.

As Clint entered the Black Jack, the three customers there looked up from their drinks, but it was the middle-aged bartender who spoke.

"Ah, no," he said, "don't be bringin' your troubles in here, Mr. Adams. Please."

"Don't worry, friend," Clint said. "I'm not going to be here for long. Just one beer."

Reluctantly the bartender drew a beer and set it on the bar.

* * *

Cutter and Aaron burst into Locksley's reception area, startling Gina. Both men stared at her.

"What are we supposed to do with her?" Aaron asked.

"Nothin'," Cutter said. "Get out!" he ordered the girl.

Gina didn't hesitate. She ran out. The two men crossed the room and slammed open the door to Locksley's office.

Husband and wife turned from the window and stared at them.

"You," Cutter said, pointing at Locksley. "Come with us."

"W-What?"

"You heard him," Aaron said. "Outside."

"B-But why?"

"Never mind," Cutter said. "Move it!"

Locksley put his hand on Angela's arm and said, "My dear—"

"Not her," Cutter said, "just you."

Angela pulled her arm out of her husband's grasp. This was obviously Tolbert's move.

"See you later, darling," she said to her husband.

"But—"

"Get him," Cutter told Billy Aaron.

Aaron crossed the room, grabbed Locksley, and shoved him toward the door. Then he turned and took a moment to look Angela up and down.

"Come on!" Cutter said.

"You're pretty," Aaron said.

"You're disgusting."

Aaron went back across the room, where he and Cutter hustled Locksley out the door and down the stairs.

"Where are we going?" he demanded as they reached the front door.

"Sheriff Tolbert thought you'd like to watch," Cutter said.

"I was going to watch," Locksley said. "From my window."

"This way," Cutter said, "you'll get a closer look."

FORTY-THREE

Tolbert saw Cutter and Aaron come out of City Hall with Locksley. He got up from his chair and walked over to them.

"What's going on, Tolbert?" Locksley demanded.

"I'm just doing what you paid me to do, boss," Tolbert said. "I'm taking care of Adams. And after him, the girl."

"Why am I down here?"

"To watch," Tolbert said. "I wanted you to have the best seat in the house."

"This is ridiculous," Locksley said. "Take me back upstairs."

"Keep him here," Tolbert told his men. "I'll bring Adams out."

"You sure you wanna do it this way, Wes?" Cutter asked.

"Just wait here with him," Tolbert said.

"Okay."

Tolbert crossed the street to the Black Jack.

* * *

Clint watched from the window, drinking his beer. When Tolbert started across, Clint had an idea what the man had in mind. Neither he nor Locksley was supposed to survive this encounter. And above, watching from the big, arched window, was Angela.

"Adams!" Tolbert called, stopping in the street just outside the Black Jack. "It's time, Adams."

Clint walked to the bar, set down the half-empty beer mug. "See? Not long at all."

"Thanks, Mr. Adams."

Clint turned and walk to the door.

From the window of her husband's office, Angela saw Clint Adams come out of the Black Jack Saloon. Tolbert was standing right there in the street. And ingeniously— she had to admit—Tolbert had managed to get her husband out on the street, too.

Her heart was racing. She was going to have to keep Tolbert around a little longer, just to satisfy the feelings she was having at that moment. The excitement was . . . heady.

Outside, Tolbert kept his eyes on the front door of the Black Jack. Finally, it opened and Clint Adams stepped out.

"What's on your mind, Sheriff?"

"I'm calling you out," Tolbert said, "in my official capacity as sheriff."

The people on either side of the street started to scramble for cover. Some simply ran into the nearest building;

others took cover behind barrels or around corners. But most of them still managed to keep an eye on the action.

Clint stepped down into the street.

"Is this where you want me, Sheriff?" he asked.

Clint started to circle to his left, causing Tolbert to circle to his right.

"Or do you want to switch sides, so you can hit Locksley with a stray bullet?"

"The center of the street is fine with me, Adams."

Clint risked a brief look at Locksley. The two backup men were standing on either side of him. But their guns were holstered.

"Now hold on!" Locksley yelled. "Just hold on a minute!"

Tolbert didn't look at Locksley, and Clint made sure to keep his eyes on Tolbert. Peripherally, he would still notice some movement from the other two.

"What's on your mind, Mr. Locksley?" Clint asked.

"This—this doesn't have to happen here now," Locksley said. "Why don't we go up to my office and talk about this?"

"But this is what you wanted, Locksley," Clint said. "You hired Tolbert to kill me."

Locksley, aware that there were townspeople watching and listening, said, "Tolbert is the sheriff now, Adams. I have no control over his actions."

"He works for you, doesn't he?"

"He works for the town."

"But you appointed him."

"Somebody had to wear the badge," Locksley argued.

"Crabtree left town. We couldn't leave the town without a lawman."

"Isn't it usually the mayor's job to appoint a new sheriff?"

"Not in this town."

"Now why doesn't that surprise me?" Clint asked.

FORTY-FOUR

"Tolbert!" Locksley shouted suddenly, abandoning his ignorance. "I order you to stop this. Do you hear me? I order it."

"Quiet him down!" Tolbert shouted.

"How dare you—"

Cutter drew his gun and stuck it in Locksley's ribs.

"You heard the man," he said. "Shut up!"

Aaron drew his gun and jammed it into Locksley on the other side.

"Yeah!"

All of Tolbert's attention was on Clint. Clint still used his peripheral vision to keep track of the others, but he was primarily focused on Tolbert.

"You really want to do this, Tolbert?"

"Really, Adams," Tolbert said. "You've been in this position many, many times before. Have you ever been able to talk anyone out of it?"

"Not that many," Clint said. "You're all pretty much the same. You think you'll get a big reputation by killing me, but you never realize that wanting and doing are two different things."

"What I want," Tolbert said, "I make happen."

"I'm curious, Wes," Clint said. "Are you actually getting paid by both of them? The husband and the wife?"

Tolbert didn't answer.

"And does Locksley know you've been poking his wife, too?"

"What?" Locksley asked. "What's tha—"

Cutter quieted him down by jamming his gun barrel into his side harder.

"All right," Tolbert said. "That's enough talking. Let's do this, Adams."

Clint turned all his attention to Tolbert.

"Whenever you're ready, Wes."

Clint watched Tolbert's eyes. In his experience, a man gave away his move by narrowing his eyes—even if it was just a fraction of an inch.

But Tolbert was good. He didn't telegraph his move that way. In fact, he didn't telegraph it at all. The man was actually as good as he thought he was.

Tolbert drew, and Clint—with nothing to give him an edge—simply had to outdraw him.

Tolbert felt that Adams was talking out of nerves. He knew he'd met his match, and was trying to put off the inevitable. Tolbert's confidence was swelling inside him, more and more each second.

No point in making Adams wait any longer.

He drew.

He thought he drew. Suddenly he couldn't feel the gun

in his hand. In fact, he couldn't feel anything except a cold sensation in his belly that quickly turned hot.

He was turning, twisting, and falling and didn't even realize that he did pull the trigger once, firing a wild shot . . .

Cutter and Aaron watched as Clint outdrew Tolbert cleanly, and killed him.

"Jesus!" Aaron said. "That was fast!"

Clint turned quickly to the two men, both of whom were holding their guns. He fired quickly, before either of them could think to pull the trigger. His actions saved Eric Locksley's life.

"Jesus!" Locksley cried out as the two men fell to the ground.

Clint first walked to Tolbert, to be sure he was dead. When he was certain, he walked to the other two. Satisfied that they, too, were dead, he ejected the empty shells from his gun and reloaded.

Locksley was still cringing between the two bodies.

People were starting to come out onto the street. Clint grabbed Locksley's arm.

"Let's go and see your wife."

He dragged Locksley into the building, and up the stairs. When they entered the office, the first thing Clint saw was the shattered glass in the big window. He hadn't known where Tolbert's wild shot had gone, but now he did.

Angela Locksley was lying on her back across her husband's desk, a bullet hole in her forehead.

"Oh, God!" Locksley said, turning his head.

"Why are you turning your head away, Locksley?" Clint asked. "I heard you and the missus weren't getting along. Guess that's why she was sleeping with Tolbert while you were sleeping with Mary Connelly."

Locksley gave Clint a murderous look. Clint put his gun barrel to the man's forehead, turning the look into one of fear.

"I can give you a matching bullet hole, so that you and your wife will look alike."

"N-No."

"I think a lot of the townspeople heard everything that was said out there," Clint said. "You're finished in this town. If there was a real sheriff in town, I'd turn you over to him."

"L-Look, Adams—"

"Now tell me you're going to leave town if I leave you alive."

"I—I'm gonna leave t-town."

"Today?"

"Today."

"I want you gone before Mary Connelly comes back," Clint said. "She and Doc are delivering a baby, and I'll want to give her the good news that she doesn't have to leave town."

Locksley nodded.

"Don't worry about your wife," Clint said, removing the gun but leaving a round circle on the man's forehead. "I'll see she's buried properly."

"Where will I go?" Locksley said.

"You might try going to see your son," Clint said, walking to the door. "You can tell him how you got his mother killed."

Watch for

THE MISSING PATRIARCH

372nd novel in the exciting GUNSMITH series
from Jove

Coming in December!

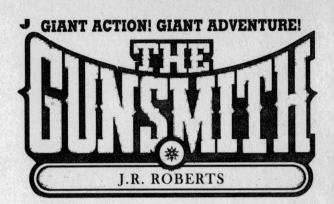

GIANT ACTION! GIANT ADVENTURE!

THE GUNSMITH

J.R. ROBERTS

penguin.com/actionwesterns

M455AS0510